# THE NICENE CIPHER

## C. G. COOPER
## MARIUS KENT

# "THE NICENE CIPHER"

*Book 1 of the Papal Justice Series*

*By C. G. Cooper*
*with Marius Kent*

**>> GET A FREE COPY OF THE CORPS JUSTICE PREQUEL SHORT STORY, *GOD-SPEED*, JUST FOR SUBSCRIBING AT HTTP://CG-COOPER.COM <<**

This is a work of fiction. Characters, names, locations and events are all products of the author's imagination. Any similarities to actual events or real persons are completely coincidental.

This novel contains violence and profanity. Readers beware.

# PROLOGUE

## BURSA, TURKEY

Mehmet Aslan's throat thumped with every beat of his heart. He walked toward the mosque, focused on placing one foot in front of the other. He paused, staring at the building, wiping the sweat from his forehead, then continued. His contact assured him the credentials he sported would survive the scrutiny of Imam Ganim—and Ganim's guard at the temple.

Said guard stiffened at Mehmet's approach and turned the submachine gun's business end toward him. Mehmet's legs went to jelly. He put both his hands up as he approached.

"Stop there," said the guard.

"Allah be praised, I come in peace," returned Mehmet. "I have a letter of introduction to Imam Ganim. If you allow me to lower my hands, I should be happy to present it to you."

"Slowly," said the guard, in a voice that shook with hair-trigger tension. "With one hand."

Mehmet lowered a hand slowly and withdrew the envelope from his coat pocket.

"Come to me, slowly, both arms raised."

He complied, somehow managing a weak smile as he approached.

"Why are you here at this hour?"

"I was told the mosque allows foreign dignitaries to stay overnight if refuge be needed. I've just arrived and I request the mosque's hospitality." He purposely used a haughty dialect and grammar, trying his best to feign the air of a scholar.

He handed the letter to the guard, who snatched it away so violently that it made Mehmet flinch.

The guard looked at the envelope, looked at him, then backed into the doorway of the mosque.

"Wait here. Keep still. Do not move or I will shoot you."

"Peace," said Mehmet. "I will not move for the love of Allah."

The guard disappeared into the shadows of the mosque. Mehmet looked around. The streets of Iznik were barren. There was a vacuum effect now, compared to the daylight hours when the place was bustling with tourists, street vendors, children at play, and social activity in the square across the street.

He snapped back to attention at the sound of the guard returning, rifle pointed at the ground.

"Please, sir, this way." He held an arm out, beckoning him to pass. "Forgive me. It is... the times."

"No matter," said Mehmet, offering the man a warm smile. He could turn on the charm at a moment's notice. Suckers like this dimwitted guard fell for it like humble peasants.

"I did not know who you were..." The guard swallowed hard, "Your Excellency."

Mehmet bowed to him in a courtly manner. He'd seen it on TV. The guard quickly exited the mosque. Mehmet heard him enter his vehicle and speed off. That elicited a calm smile.

Mehmet removed his shoes and entered the main room. He squinted through the darkness to the Mihrab niche on the opposite side and smiled again.

*Salvation lay beneath the stone,* he thought.

"My dear," said Imam Ganim, approaching with hands clasped before him. "I am terribly sorry for your mistreatment. Our guard is, well, he's very good, you see. We've been lucky in that—"

"Do you have what I need?" Mehmet said forcefully, the time for courtesy gone.

The imam's lower lip trembled. "Indeed," he said in a measured tone. "It arrived earlier. I signed for it myself."

Mehmet took a step closer to him, savoring the terror in the man's eyes. "Then get out of here, you swine."

The imam's eyes widened. "How dare you talk to me in this way, and in a sacred place!"

"I don't care about your sacred place. You got your money. Leave." He stared at the trembling figure before him.

Timidly, the imam walked past him. He stopped at the door to gather his shoes, and then turned. "Don't..." His dry throat clicked and he paused. "Don't do too much... damage. I implore you."

"You got your money, old man. Get out, or I'll bury your corpse when I'm done."

The imam needed no further prodding. He left in a rush.

Mehmet Aslan removed his coat and bounded up the flight of stairs to his right. The imam's office door was open. Inside, a rented jackhammer lay amongst the marble and jade-colored tiles – a jagged piece of ugliness in this beautiful place.

He did his deed, which took him an hour. He was a little worried about the noise alerting the neighborhood, having placed his trust in the thickness of the walls and nothing else. He finished, sweaty and panting and holding his treasure.

And when he left the mosque, his contact was standing out front, leaning against the fender of a running vehicle.

Mehmet chuckled nervously. "I didn't hear you pull up. I-I thought we agreed to meet at the predetermined location."

"I changed my mind," said the man.

Two others emerged from the car.

Two more coalesced from behind.

One put a cloth over Mehmet's mouth. Something sickly and sweet entered his nostrils.

Mehmet Aslan bucked to no avail. The fatigue swallowed him to the point of rigidity. He knew he was in a car. And then he knew he was in a warehouse, or was it an alleyway? Or was it his hometown, in his bedroom, hearing his father beating his mother?

Then, there was a chainsaw. And there was only the color red...

A priest, a rabbi, and an archeologist walked into a bar.

"Yeah, gimme three shots of J&B," said the archeologist. "And for you gentlemen?"

A white and a red zinfandel. Who knows who got which. Tom Dempsey had already scoped out a table in the far corner and was on his way there. Dempsey didn't wait for the other two to sit before downing the shots, taking breaths in between like a swimmer.

Father Norman and Rabbi Schlochem sat down.

"Dammit," Tom said, staring at the empty glasses, "I should have ordered a chaser."

"I get the feeling something's bothering you," said Father Norman. He stared at Dempsey. Stared *through* him.

"Stop that, will you?"

"Stop what?"

"You're staring at me. I don't like it. Feels like I'm in confession."

"Are you?"

"Very funny."

"Would you two like to be alone?" asked the rabbi.

"No," said Dempsey. "That's alright. I need you here. Both of you. You're gonna think this is crazy, but you're the only two I can trust."

The two holy men exchanged glances.

"Go on," said Dempsey, "sip your damn wine. You're gonna need it. And we're gonna be here a while." He snapped his fingers at the server as she passed. She gave him a look and kept walking.

"Broads," he said, exasperated. "What's it like not having to deal with them, Father?"

"What's on your mind, Tom?"

The middle-aged archeologist chuckled. The booze was already hitting his head and he liked it. The muscles in his stomach relaxed a hair. He put both hands on the table, palms down. "OK. You ready? I've got a problem."

There was a moment of uncomfortable silence among the three men. Surrounding them was the din of Friday night happy hour, and some song by a chick with one name being sung poorly by a female couple engaged in drunk karaoke.

"Well?" the priest asked impatiently.

"That's it."

The rabbi opened his hands. "That's it?"

"That's it."

"You brought us here to tell us you have a problem?"

"Correctamundo."

The holy men exchanged glances again.

"Are we supposed to guess?" said Father Norman.

"Nope."

"Well then," said the rabbi, "cheers." He clinked the priest's glass and took a sip.

Dempsey breathed deeply. Father Norman was staring again.

"OK. You want more? You see, the thing is, I can't really tell you more."

"Can you give us a hint?" questioned the rabbi, leaning in, annoyed with Dempsey's antics.

"No. What I'm saying is, I can't tell you any more until I get a promise. From both of you."

"Such as?"

"I need you, Father, to treat this as if it really is the confessional. And I know you really can't do that with the rabbi here, so I need you to swear yourself to secrecy. And you, Rabbi, need to swear to secrecy as well. Only then will I tell you my problem."

The priest took a long sip of his wine. Red or white zin, Dempsey couldn't tell in the dimness of the bar.

A server appeared at their table as if he'd materialized out of nowhere. "Hi there, my name is Phillip, I'll be taking care of you tonight. I see you have your drinks. Can I start you gentlemen off with anything? Jalapeno poppers or potato skins?"

"Double J&B, no ice," Dempsey said to the table.

"OK. Double J&B, no ice. Do you want to order food now, or do you need a minute to decide?"

Dempsey pursed his lips. "I decided. Another double J&B. No ice."

"O-K," said the waiter. "I'll be right back."

"This is on me, by the way," said Dempsey. "Drink up."

"Please get to the point," said Rabbi Schlochem, once the waiter left.

Dempsey rubbed his temples. "Alright. I made a discovery last week. In Iznik."

"Iznik?" asked the rabbi. "That's in Turkey?"

"Congratulations, Rabbi. You win a gold unicorn turd."

The priest leaned in and said sharply, "That's *enough*, Tom."

"Oh, the old headmaster rears his ugly head. Sorry, I haven't had anything to eat since last night. The booze... *whew*... anyway. Where was I?"

"Turkey," said Rabbi Schlochem. "You made a discovery."

"Yes, that's right. Father, how good's your biblical lore?"

"Is that supposed to be a joke?"

Dempsey scrunched his eyes shut. Words were failing him. Three shots in and he was snockered.

"No, dammit. Sorry. I mean, how well do you know your biblical *history*?"

"I know the stories like the back of my—"

Dempsey clenched his fists. "No, no, listen. Not the stories. I mean, what's *behind* the stories. How they got into the Bible."

The rabbi turned his head to the priest.

"I suppose," said Father Norman, "I know a little."

"Ah huh," said Dempsey. "And you, Rabbi?"

"I know some. Probably less that this distinguished fellow to my left."

"Ah huh. Well, do you know what they used to call Izquick? Bizquick...?" He put his head in his hand.

At this moment, the waiter placed a napkin on the table and a drink on top of it. Rabbi Schlochem immediately grabbed it and placed it on the edge of the table between himself and Father Norman. "Take it easy," he said.

Dempsey spoke in measured tones. "Do either of you know what Iznik used to be called?"

The men shook their heads.

"It used to be known as *Nicaea*. Ring a bell, Father?"

The priest nodded. "It does."

"Nicaea," said the rabbi. "Isn't that—?"

"The Nicene creed," said Father Norman.

"A unicorn turd for this biblicalonian theologianista over here!"

"Get on with it, Tom."

"Rabbi," said Dempsey, "our friend is being very rude. Nicaea is more than just a namesake to a creed that millions of the faithful recite every Sunday. It happens to be the historic home of the Council of Nicaea. Do you know what transpired at the council in 325 A.D.?"

"I admit my ignorance."

"Father?"

The priest began speaking, not taking his eyes off the inebriated man. "It was an ecumenical council convened under the auspices of Emperor Constantine. They'd reached a consensus, after three hundred years of dispute. Resolved certain... Christological issues. Christ's divinity, the nature of the Holy Trinity, Easter observance, *et cetera*."

"You're forgetting something," Dempsey sang. "The Nicene creed?"

"Well, yes, of course. That goes without saying."

"Rabbi," said Dempsey, "in just a couple of dozen phrases, the Nicene creed encompasses the entirety of the Catholic faith. One God, the Father; His Son, begotten, not made; and all those other wonderful things. Died for your sins, blah blah blah. So, you remember last year I went and I got myself a grant? And it was just in a nick of time because I found out Doris was cheating on me with that meathead adjunct from the Psych Department who couldn't wait to get her on the couch and teach her Freud from Jung, if you know what I mean. The little slut was fired and publicly shamed and yours truly went to Turkey. Hooray for our team, right? So, I get there and things are going pretty great. The air is nice. The food's tasty. And I get to play in the sand, which I love more than life itself. And then, my little team hits pay dirt. I'm not too proud to say that it was my direction that made it possible. They said not to dig there because it'd already been dug up, you know? But I told them to dig anyway. Because I had a hunch, you see. And you tell me what scientific breakthrough *didn't* have its origin in the hunch of some poor schmuck with nothing better to do with his time and I'll give you a kiss right on the mouth."

"Get on with your story, Tom."

"Give me a drink first."

"Get on with it."

"Fine. So we dug it up. And we found something. And it's hidden now someplace safe. Because it's something really, really bad."

All ambient noise seemed to fade away. Dempsey's audience was rapt. He grabbed his drink effortlessly and took a nice, burning swig.

"I found something, gentlemen, that can undo millennia."

The rabbi's eyes narrowed. "What did you find?"

"A letter," Dempsey said, unable to keep his voice from shaking. "From Simon Magus to Saint Paul. Yes, *that* Saint Paul."

The priest was stunned into silence.

Dempsey smiled. "You didn't think anyone ever wrote him back, did you?"

"What kind of letter?" asked Father Norman, clutching his wine glass as if he was about to be in sudden need of it.

"*The* letter, Father. The Nicene Cipher."

In the dimness of a dive bar, the Catholic priest went white.

---

RABBI SCHLOCHEM WASN'T crazy about the way his friend had downed his glass of wine in one shot and left for the car they'd driven in. Father Norman refused to speak with him as the priest pulled away from the bar and started off. Schlochem tolerated the priest's eccentricity like he tolerated their dogmatic differences: cautiously.

When they were safely on their way back to the rectory that Father Norman called home, driving along Route 4 by themselves on a long stretch of road with no lights, the priest finally spoke.

"Why did Tom want us to meet him in such an out-of-the-way place? God help us all."

"Do you mind telling me what that was all about?"

"It was probably nothing."

The rabbi couldn't suppress his laughter. "John, anyone ever tell you you're a rotten liar?"

The priest sighed heavily. "What I mean is, I overreacted and I'm embarrassed. The Nicene Cipher is a myth. I should have known better than to put any weight into Tom's story."

"You know him well enough."

"I do."

"How long ago did you teach him at seminary?"

The priest let out a mouthy gust of breath. "Ohhh, it's gotta be about fifteen years now?"

"So you *knew* him well enough. Fifteen years is a long time. A lot can happen to change a man, especially one who abandoned his calling."

"Listen, the priesthood isn't for everyone. Anyway, you're right, I have no reason to put any stock in what he said."

"But if you did?" asked the rabbi, knowing full well that he was provoking his friend into confession.

"Then... I'd be very worried. Simon Magus was a heretic who inspired another heretic by the name of Marcion of Sinope. Marcion had a lot of... Let's just say his views of God and Jesus didn't exactly conform with what we in the faith understand to be the true revelation."

"John, it's me. You're talking like I'm one of your students."

"The Nicene Cipher is a mysterious document that supposedly contains the *one true* revelation as to the nature of Christ. Marcion refers to it in a bit of writing that was later deemed a forgery. But recent evidence suggests that it was only deemed so because of the inflammatory nature of it."

"And I suppose that Marcion's revelation differs from the Catholic Church's official position?"

"It does. Significantly. It scared the Church into suppressing it."

"John, for argument's sake, let's just imagine that such a document were to be used in, say, a political way. Say it were to be verified as a statement of fact."

The priest didn't answer.

"John?"

"David," said Father Norman, "if we suddenly found out that Shakespeare really didn't write all his plays—that it was the Earl of Devonshire or Queen Elizabeth or Christopher Marlowe that was the true author—I would be OK with that. It would change nothing of the plays. We'd still have them in all their magnificent glory. But prove to me that the essential truths revealed in the Catholic faith through St. Paul are a falsehood, and that's the end of it. I no longer have a purpose. And if I don't, then neither does anyone else. You mentioned what happens politically? Politically, it's a catastrophe. You think the world's in a mess now with its religious differences—"

He broke off and fell silent for the remainder of the drive, staring out the window.

Rabbi David Schlochem had enough intellect to process what his friend had said, and to know not to press the matter further. Not tonight. They had time to think on it. At least that's what he thought.

# BURSA, TURKEY

Ridley Shane emerged from a maze of narrow streets lined with ramshackle flats to an oasis of palm trees. For all he knew, he'd reached Southern California.

Yeşil Camii, the famed "Green Mosque," appeared in the distance. Though impressive in its architecture, it wasn't as imposing as he thought it would be. He was looking for grandiosity, not a building that, were it not for the dome and minaret, could have doubled as a welcome center.

He parked his car near a paved outdoor seating area located across the street. He was done with driving. It was a short walk to the place of worship.

The seating area was immaculately clean. It culminated in a tiny playground with a single, multicolored tube slide, a swing set with fading red and yellow paint, and nothing else, located on a swatch of mostly bare lawn between walkways. The playground had been a hasty afterthought. There were no kids anywhere near it.

He padded across the street to the mosque. It loomed a bit larger here, yet was still unassuming, situated as it was a short walk away from a litter of ancient ruins and tumbled pillars. He wished he'd read a little more on the history of the place.

The entrance to the narthex of the mosque, lacking the usual portico, was blocked off with police tape. Ridley handed his pass to the guard, who eyed him suspiciously. The man muttered something in Arabic, then handed the pass back to him and lifted the police tape slightly, a show of good faith.

Ridley paused at the entrance, removed his shoes, and entered.

It was his first time inside a mosque. He wasn't sure what to expect. Take your pick from any one of a number of the famous Catholic churches and cathedrals in the world, and Ridley, the consummate spiritual searcher, could give a fairly detailed description (when pressed for it) of the opulence of Catholic veneration. Like all good Catholics, he approved of the opulence of Catholic places of worship as measuring up to their authority and Holy Truth, but felt sufficient shame in them as well. It was all part of the dichotomy of religious mystery, this balancing of values and actual, real-time practice.

The exterior of the building belied the enormity of the interior. Perhaps it would have seemed underwhelming in size were it not for the high-domed ceiling, supported by columns (Corinthian – Who knew?), the magnificent stone archways through which one had to pass in order to enter, and the masonry of the Mihrab niche at the opposite end of the room; not to mention the incredible ten-pointed chandelier that hung in the direct center of the hall. This was the entirety of the building's interior, if you didn't count the outdoor "*sahn*" courtyard.

Ridley stepped across the blue-green carpet toward the niche, where several police officers and military men stood, shoeless, discussing something in hushed tones.

"Mr. Shane," whispered a Middle Eastern man with a thick English accent, "very good of you to come."

Ridley nodded and shook the man's hand. The man waited for a reciprocal verbal greeting; when he realized he wasn't going to get it, he sprung into diplomacy. "Sorry. I am Emin Sadik, United States Ambassador to Turkey. We spoke on the phone... *several times.*"

Ridley smiled in recognition of the name and voice.

"President Zimmer thought it best I show you around personally." The man stepped aside to allow Ridley to stand next to him. He said, "Please, let us through."

The entourage of policemen and military parted, and Ridley saw the object of their attention: a hole in the floor of the mosque, measuring about two and a half feet in diameter.

Ridley looked around. "How do you use a jackhammer in here without alerting the locals?"

"Or the guard and the imam," said a police officer, his English colored by a Turkish accent.

"Where are they?" said Ridley.

"We're still trying to figure that out at the moment. Excuse me, but is there a reason for this American to be here?

"Mr. Shane is here as a favor to us granted by the American government," explained Sadik.

"I repeat," said the officer, "this is not a matter of international diplomacy."

Ridley took out his cell phone and brought up a picture of a dead man.

The policeman winced at the bloody sight, and then looked at Ridley incredulously.

Ridley put away the phone. "That is, or was," he said, "a professor of religious archeology by the name of Martin Schell. He was here on visa, studying abroad."

"What is the point?" the policeman asked indignantly, having composed himself.

"He was stabbed to death two nights ago in his hotel room. Whoever did it was searching for something."

"Evidently," said Sadik, "they found it. It was a floor plan that matched the layout of this mosque."

"I'm confused," said the cop. "Are you saying whoever killed that man is responsible for this desecration?"

"That's what we believe," said Sadik.

"Then you have the man who did this."

"Part of him," said Ridley.

"What do you mean, 'part of him'?"

Sadik looked at Ridley, then moistened his lips. "We found his head. The map was stapled to it."

"Good God," muttered the cop.

"I'll spare you the photo," said Ridley. "Whoever's behind the killings had no particular desire to conceal the nature of the crimes. They were only interested in committing them."

"And do you know who committed them?"

Ridley shook his head.

"Not yet," Sadik clarified.

"Once again," said the cop, "is this really a matter for the American government?"

"Martin Schell was a military veteran studying archeology under the G.I. Bill. He's an American citizen. He's also the son of Senator Michael Schell of Illinois. So yes, this is a matter for the American government."

The policeman rubbed his brow. "You mentioned a moment ago that someone ordered these crimes. Do you have any idea as to who that might be?"

"Not yet," said Ridley

"And who is the owner of the head?"

"His name was Mehmet Aslan," said Sadik.

"Is he being investigated?"

"He is and was," said Ridley. "We still don't know how he fits in. He's got some prior run-ins with the law. Petty theft. Gang-related violence."

The terse Ridley Shane stared at the niche, contemplating something.

Sadik cleared his throat. "Er, well then, I guess Mr. Shane has seen enough of this, er, scene."

Ridley nodded.

"Very well. Gentleman."

Ridley and Sadik parted company with the group and exited the mosque, waiting until they were off holy grounds before discussing what they'd withheld from Turkish authorities.

"Well?" said Sadik.

"Well what?"

"You think it was wise not to tell them about the rest of Mehmet's body?"

"Yes."

Sadik looked up and down the narrow road. "Where did you park?"

"Across the street. Through here."

They crossed the sparse children's playground into the outdoor seating area.

"And you think," said Sadik, "that it's really enough to concern... *him?*"

Ridley nodded. "Yes."

"Oh dear."

They said nothing else to one another, other than a curt good-bye. And Ridley got into his car. He took out his phone, found the picture of Mehmet Aslan's headless body that they'd found three blocks over from the hotel where Martin Schell had been murdered. He pursed his lips. There was nothing otherwise remarkable about the picture. It was visual death in a slum alley-way, meaningless and disgusting. He swiped once and stared at the close-up photo he'd taken of the body. A small note had been stapled to the exposed chest. The handwriting was in the process of being analyzed, though he had no expectations about that. He knew it would reveal nothing useful. What *was* of use was the context of the message:

*"So it goes with all 'holy' institutions: Once the head is severed, the body, the vessel of evil, crumbles back into dust."*

Placing the word holy in quotes was a key. But what was more telling to Ridley was the word *dust*.

According to Muslims, God–Allah—created Adam from a clot of blood. Man's origin from dust was strictly a Judeo-Christian idea. Desecration of the mosque was bad enough, but to have it be inferred that such desecration was part of a direct threat to Islam was like tossing a cigarette butt into a jet fuel refinery. No one could risk such inference. Best to keep it under wraps until the mystery was solved. Especially since another part of the letter seemed to threaten the Church itself. Although it wasn't directly provable, judging from radical atheist literature found in Aslan's flea-infested apartment, *head* might be a reference to the pope; and *body*, to the Catholic faith itself. Maybe it was a longshot, but Ridley couldn't afford to let it go. He closed his camera roll and dialed a number no one but a privileged few possessed.

About 1500 miles away, a phone rang in the Vatican office.

## TILLINGS NECK, NY

Tom Dempsey sloshed into his living room and collapsed onto the couch. Driving home was idiotic, but he hadn't had enough money for a cab, not after the fifty bucks he'd dropped on drinks.

The room swam in a swirl before him. But there was the gnawing fear in his gut that had plagued him ever since returning home from Turkey. He didn't like the idea that the cipher was in the hands of that kid Schell. Schell was too inexperienced, too haphazard with his priorities. But it was the safest place the item could be, he reminded himself. Schell was the son of a United States Senator. In other words, he was untouchable. And he'd had enough worldly experience to know where not to tread in the old city. Most importantly, the kid knew how to keep his mouth shut.

Still, the fear remained.

He got up from the couch. The room spun on its axis.

"Woooooo boy..." he said, regaining his balance. He made his way to the liquor cabinet. Summer nighttime, windows open. Neighbors arguing about money. She wants to spend it on paying down the credit cards. Meanwhile, he's frittering it away on manly trinkets.

"Calm down, already," Dempsey muttered. "God, you guys are worse than leaf blowers." He grabbed a bottle of Dewar's. "Ah well. It's better than battery acid." Poured himself a shot and downed it, standing, open bottle in hand.

"Mr. Dempsey," said a male voice.

Dempsey spun, sending the bottle shattering to the floor. He looked down at his feet, then back up from his intruder.

"A vaste of vhiskey," he said, his pronunciation of w's as v's betraying the Turkish origin of his accent.

"Who are you?"

"A friend of a friend. I'm sorry to intrude. It looks as though you vere in the midst of celebrating."

"What do you want?"

"Relax, Mr. Dempsey. May I sit?"

The man did so without waiting for a reply. He was of medium-build, dressed in a beautifully tailored business suit. He was clean-shaven, free of blemishes like a model. He smiled close-mouthed and somewhat crookedly, and he smelled vaguely of a tobacco-scented cologne. He reminded Dempsey of a young movie studio executive.

"This is a dreadful place you live in. It's temporary, I hope?"

Dempsey, unmoving. "What do you want?"

"I vant to talk to you about your recent discowery."

"What about it?"

"Who vere you meeting vith tonight?"

"None of your damn business."

The man smiled. Crooked mouth. "Religious men, no?"

"Leave now, before I call the cops."

"I don't vant to leave, Mr. Dempsey. I vant us to talk a bit. I could have killed you without you knowing, vhile you vere drinking. Vhy vould I vant to kill you now? Please, have a seat."

Dempsey stepped over the puddle of whiskey, feeling the

crunch of broken bottle shrapnel the entire way toward the easy chair across from his intruder.

"I vant to talk to you about how you managed such a rare find," the man said in an oily voice. "It's a vonderful piece of vork."

"I don't know what you're talking about."

"Oh, but I vant to know. I represent certain interested parties."

"Like whom?"

"Whom? I'm afraid I'm not at liberty to say. But I assure you, these parties have a great deal of influence, and are not adwerse to compensating you for your troubles."

"What troubles?"

"The troubles you are most certainly to run into being the holder of such—forgive me—wolatile information. Already there have been complications. Such complications can easily lead to your doorstep, Mr. Dempsey."

"As they already have."

The man smiled. "Entrust this information to me, Mr. Dempsey, and this matter, like the prowerbial cup, vill pass from your lips."

"Stick it up your granddaddy's ass." The booze was weighing him down like a lead sheet.

The man rose from the couch. "I can't reason vith you, then?"

"You're going to kill me," said Dempsey, suddenly numb. "Do it already."

"I told you," said the man, "I didn't come here with that intention."

At that moment, a pair of hands appeared from behind Dempsey's chair. And a piece of piano wire cut into his neck.

## COMMACK, NY

Father John Norman couldn't sleep. It was three o'clock in the morning. He thought of the way his favorite author, Ray Bradbury, once put it: "Three a.m... you're the nearest to dead you'll ever be save dying."

He got up and paced his tiny furnished room in the rectory. He'd considered shooting a few hoops in the court behind the house, but he was still relatively new at the parish, being on loan as he was, and the other priests had already found him a bit odd. Why complicate matters? He threw on casual vestments and left the rectory to take a drive.

As the evergreens along Route 4 swished by in a blur, he let his mind wander to the hazy recollections of his encounter with Tom Dempsey. And one question in particular: What if Tom's story was true?

All his life, Father Norman was a man of two minds. There was his rational mind, the one that liked to view the world in terms of science and empirical truth; and, diametrically opposed to that, his religious mind. He was comfortable with the two forces, preferring to think of them as evidence of the Divine in man. He'd often asked of his students: What would man be without this struggle? One had to experience a dark night of the soul, he insisted, even if the night lasted a lifetime.

And so, with literal darkness ahead, and with literal lights lighting his way, he contemplated the question: What if Tom's story was true?

If that was the case, something had to be done. This was his gut response. This was his rational mind conquered by his mind of faith, which was inevitably the stronger one.

And then there was the other question: Why *him*? There had to be a reason Dempsey chose his old seminary professor to be the recipient of this colossal secret. He hadn't really kept in close contact with Dempsey for a while now. A couple of emails here and there. And of course there was that time Father Norman attended a symposium on the religious significance of certain archeological finds unearthed near Jerusalem, and was surprised to find his old seminary student chairing the panel discussion. It was there that he met Rabbi Schlochem, and the three enjoyed an evening of nightcaps and philosophical discussion back at Dempsey's modest flat.

Over time, as these things often do, the emails trickled to a complete stop. Then out of the blue came the harried message from Dempsey all but demanding to see him and the rabbi. (The former student had read in the local newspaper about Father Norman's recent transfer to a parish just outside of Tillings Neck.)

So again, why him?

He knew why, of course, in his heart. Dempsey wanted Father Norman to reach out to his cousin, Emilio Garcia, known to the world as Pope Leo XIV.

There could be no other reason.

But he had to be sure. He took the exit off Route 4 that would lead him to his answer.

THE HOUSE, a boxy, folk Victorian, looked like it had given up on life. Ramshackle and stained with the juices of long-gone vegetation, it wasn't the place that Father Norman remembered. But it was the same house nonetheless. Dempsey had obviously spent months away at a stretch without hiring anyone to care for the place.

There was a slight hill leading up to the front porch, with a path of stone steps cut into it. Father Norman had only to reach the base of these to realize that something was terribly wrong: the door was open, and the house was completely dark.

As he ascended, a heavy hesitation in his steps, he surmised that it truly was difficult to see the open door from the road with the lights off within. Street lamps were spread out every four houses or so, and Dempsey's was one of the ones smack dab in the dark.

A screech of tires made his head whirl around just in time to see a car taking off down the road, its lights coming on only when it reached the end of the block.

He crept up to the doorway.

"Tom?"

No answer.

He pushed the door open. His eyes had adjusted to the darkness enough to notice that something was lying in a heap on the floor in the middle of the living room.

He called out, "Tom?"

A metallic smell in the room made his stomach turn.

His fingers found a lamp switch.

Dempsey's severed head lay at his feet.

He could have screamed. He was about to. But something heavy smashed into the back of his head. He barely felt the series of blows before he lost consciousness.

# TILLINGS NECK, NY

"Anyone talking?" Chief Detective Maddox asked over the police tape. He was the last to arrive, having received the call in the middle of a late-night run for Cool Ranch Doritos (family-sized) in order to satiate the prenatal craving of his insomniac wife.

Detective Warren Little answered, "We got a witness who thinks he saw a sedan take off down the block without headlights. A couple of neighbors reported hearing tires screeching. Our headlights guy lives right across the street. He saw someone lurking around the front of the house."

"What was he doing up?"

"Wife is pregnant."

Maddox rolled his eyes. "I feel his pain."

He stepped into the house. Among the millings-about of a dozen police and forensic staff lay two bodies, both separated from their heads.

"God," muttered Maddox. "What the hell happened?"

"One discovered the other. Perp was obviously still lingering."

Maddox narrowed his eyes at the closer of the two bodies. "Priest?"

"Looks like it."

He sighed. "Alright. Let's get it done. Need anything?"

Detective Little shook his head. "We're good."

Maddox was about to step away when an officer sauntered up to Little with a mini laptop propped on his forearm. "I think I found him."

"The priest?" said Maddox.

"He's Father John Joseph Norman. Graduated Immaculate Conception Seminary in 1982. His record lists next of kin as a Father Emilio Garcia, Archbishop of Argentina, of all people."

"Sure it's him?" said Little.

"Put it against his ID. Birthday's a match."

"Hang on," said Maddox. Something ignited in his brain. "Father *who* in Argentina?"

"Emilio Garcia?" said the cop.

"Huh. Does it list the relation?"

"Just says, 'cousin'."

A bewildered chuckle came from his chest.

"Sir?" said Little.

"No, it's just... that's, I mean, I'm pretty sure that's the pope."

"The pope? As in the... the *pope* pope?"

Maddox took out his phone and Googled Pope Leo XIV. "Yeah, that's him." He looked at the officer with the laptop. "You find anyone else?"

"No, sir."

"Keep looking. Otherwise..."

"Sir?"

Maddox shrugged. "Otherwise we contact the pope."

---

AFTER AN HOUR, both bodies were tagged and bagged. The

officer with the laptop—Maddox later found out he was a rookie by the name of Abeles—walked up to him.

"Detective Little said you might want to see this. I did a search on Pope Leo's family, came up with something interesting. Found cousins by the name of Garcia located in the tristate area. Matched them to the Norman family, also in the tristate area. I'll do a little more searching, but it looks like these Normans may be the guy's immediate family. The people search on them lists a Father John J. Norman as possibly related."

"Alrighty, we might have our priest. Nice job."

Maddox spotted Little leaning on Tom Dempsey's kitchen counter.

"Whatcha got?"

"Photos. Nothing crazy. Guy was an archeologist. We got a ton of pictures here of him up to his neck in pottery and all sorts of stuff. I don't see any loved ones anywhere. Not on the mantle. Not on the nightstand. Guy was flying solo."

"What do you think the priest has to do with him?"

"That's what I'm trying to find out. I think the guy who our neighbor saw lurking outside may have been the priest. What he was coming here for in the middle of the night is anyone's guess."

"You think it's...?"

Little met his eyes. A smirk appeared on his face. "It looks that way, but I don't want to jump to any conclusions. We had a priest scandal here about six years ago, remember? Just relax. We don't need to cause a moral panic." He looked at Maddox, straightening. "With all due respect, sir."

"Easy. It's alright. I'm gonna head back to the station. Looks like I'm not getting any sleep for the next forty-eight."

"Sure. Oh, hey, before I forget..." Little walked past the chief detective, motioning for him to follow. "You'll like this. Take a look at that typewriter on the desk."

"Typewriter? Who uses a manual typewriter anymore?"

"He did apparently. We found something pretty crazy typed there. Probably the perp. And before you ask, no, the fingerprints on the keys were wiped."

Maddox leaned over the antique machine and squinted at the paper rolled within. A paragraph of what looked to be academic writing had broken off. There were a few blank spaces, and then the cryptic phrase: *So it goes with all 'holy' institutions. Once the head is severed, the body, the vessel of evil, crumbles back into dust.*

Maddox stood up. "I want this thing put under a microscope until we find something. Understand?"

"Yes, sir."

"And let me know the minute you talk to the priest's family." He paused. "His family *here*."

"Yes, sir."

Chief Richard Maddox stepped out of the house into the hazy dawn and took a breath.

Three days later, Pope Leo XIV received a call from his family in America.

# VATICAN CITY, ITALY

L ike everyone else, Ridley Shane never lost his sense of awe upon entering Vatican City. As he took the exit off the Via di Porta Cavalleggeri, he put his finger over the pause button on the audiobook he was listening to. He let the speaker finish the sentence first:

> *"One is certainly capable of having a sense of the transcendent without believing in being aware of the presence of God. But it is only with this awareness that transcendence has applicable meaning."*

It was a good breaking point. The book, *Jacob's Escalator, the Power of Belief in the Modern Age*, had been recommended to him by a friend. It was the perfect material for a drive into Vatican City, the road to which is paved with wide streets, outlets, storage facilities, and every other aspect of modern, secular life. Ridley, with his interest in all things spiritual, immersed himself in the words of the author, who advocated a more strident belief system as being all the more necessary in the Information Age.

Ridley had been summoned here by Pope Leo himself, though

not directly. Once again, it was President Zimmer who'd intervened. The pope had an urgent matter that needed attention, and it happened to be the kind of attention that Ridley Shane was especially keen in giving. Zimmer had hinted at Ridley's possible collaboration with the Brotherhood. "Just meet with the guy," Zimmer had told him. "He'll let you know in no uncertain terms whether you'll be working it alone."

As he pulled up to the fifty-foot wall that guarded the only vehicular entrance into Vatican City, he fished out his special ID badge, a set of three plastic cards with swipe strips, connected by a ring through a hole in the corner. He waited patiently while a guard, without a single word, separated the cards and swiped all three on a portable computer. After a moment, there was a barely audible beep. The guard looked at Ridley's face, then wordlessly handed him a biometric sensor the size of a matchbook. Ridley took it between his thumb and forefinger and waited, staring ahead at the magnificence of the city that lay before him. Another beep. He handed the sensor back to the guard, who in turn handed his badge back to him, neatly re-clipped.

Ridley drove on, barely avoiding a collision with a careening tour bus along the way. The dome of St. Peter's Basilica ahead, like a beacon, stood in majesty above all. He rounded the turn onto Via di Porta Angelica, and then a right onto Borgo Pio, where he found a parking garage next to a pizzeria. His stomach grumbled at the thought of it. Later. That would be his reward for a job well done, he promised himself.

He walked the short way down Borgo Pio, crossed the street where he had turned, and continued onto the pedestrian-only Via Sant'Anna. A Swiss guard watched him pass as he made his way to the Papal Apartments complex of the massive Apostolic Palace.

"RIDLEY," cried Pope Leo, arms outstretched.

Ridley took his hand and kissed the ring.

"Stop that at once," said the holy man.

"Your Eminence," said Ridley.

"And none of that. We're friends. Can we get you anything? Tea? Coffee?"

"Water?"

Pope Leo looked over his shoulder and smiled. Ridley turned around to see a servant who could have been a statue move from the wall to the door, presumably to fetch the beverage.

"I don't like having to do that," the pope remarked.

"Do what? Get water?"

"No, send a servant. They get paid to do it, but it's so... privileged. I come from a poor family. And our Lord possessed nothing but the clothes on his back and the sandals on his feet. And here I am in a world of riches." He stared at Ridley for a moment. "You're emotionally burdened."

*How does he do that?* Ridley wondered, and not for the first time. It was impossible not to be awed by the man standing in front of him. "That and I'm starving."

"You should have said so. Let us get you—"

"I'd rather nourish the spirit first."

The pope smiled and sat down at the large office desk. "Please," he said, indicating a seat. When Ridley was seated, the pope said, "Ask."

"Why?"

The servant returned with a silver tray containing a carafe of water and two crystal tumblers.

"You can leave that right here," said the holy man, tapping the edge of the desk. The servant bowed her head and did as he asked. "And would you excuse us?" Another bow.

The door to the office closed behind them.

"Why?" Ridley repeated.

"A series of crimes have been committed. Three you know about, two you don't."

"The murders in Turkey."

"And the theft and desecration," the pope said with a nod. "They are, of course, linked. And with them, there have been two murders in America. One of them was my cousin."

"I'm very sorry to hear that. Please accept my condolences."

"Thank you. He wasn't alone. There was another body at the scene. Both bodies were..." he gestured with his hands, as if searching in vain for a euphemism, "... beheaded."

Ridley nodded his head in reverence. "I'm sorry."

The pope's face was grave. "You found a note at the scene of a similar murder. Something referencing the 'head'. This same note, word for word, was found at the scene of my cousin's untimely death. When you originally notified my office of the first murder, I have to admit I was skeptical. It was a bit of a stretch, as you Americans say. Now that a member of my family is involved, my skepticism has, alas, withered somewhat."

"I'm going to assume they haven't caught the culprit?"

"Not yet. Something you said intrigued me, however. The reference in the note to 'dust'. The crimes committed did appear to be directed at the Muslim faith, but it seems now that this is a crime against the Catholic Church."

"Do you have a theory?"

"It's not Muslim radicals, otherwise they would not have desecrated a mosque."

"It could have been a radical sect."

Something was weighing on the pope's conscience. His face, now turned toward the desk, was brooding, searching. He sighed once, heavily. "We did a bit more research. Mehmet Aslan, the man whose body you found, was an atheist."

"OK. That changes the picture slightly. You think this was part of some radical atheistic agenda?

"No."

"And your reason?"

"Because of Tom Dempsey, the other victim in America. He was conducting an archeological expedition in Turkey. There he came across a map. Our sources, working in congruence with the CIA, have uncovered a money trail that leads directly to Aslan from a Swiss bank account. We're working to uncover where the money originated, but we believe Tom Dempsey made the deposit. In the meantime, Martin Schell, a student to whom Tom Dempsey entrusted the map, was found murdered by Aslan."

"A neat little web."

"Here is where it gets a bit more complicated. We've been able to contact a certain Rabbi David Schlochem, a mutual friend of Tom Dempsey and my cousin. The rabbi tells us that Dempsey was in a panic over having made a discovery in Turkey of a certain artifact, an ancient letter. Now, this is quite different terminology —'map' as opposed to 'letter'. We think that Dempsey hired Aslan to desecrate the mosque in order to obtain the supposed letter, which was buried beneath the niche."

Ridley rubbed his eyes and poured himself a tumbler of water.

"I told you it gets complicated," the pope said, offering his own glass to be filled.

"I have a feeling there's more."

The pope took a deep breath. "The letter," he said, looking graver than before.

"What about it?"

"If it exists, it could be... very damaging."

"How so?"

"It could destroy the Church."

The words fell heavy in the room. Ridley took a sip of the

water, which was clean and cool, and thought for a minute. "Tell me why."

"I thought you'd never ask. But before I do," he said, leaning forward, his palms flat upon the surface of the desk, "I need to summon the Brothers."

Ridley took a steadying breath and leaned back in his chair.

It was gonna be *that* kind of job.

# VATICAN CITY

They convened in the pope's private garden, each in the garb of their shared calling.

The group was merely the latest incarnation of an elite force dedicated to defending the faith. The Brothers of St. Longinus were the best of the best, each in an unmatched class, all experts in tactical military skill and espionage. They had taken an oath to protect the Holy Office, in the name of God, at all costs.

This top-secret group of monks were sitting around with pints of Trappist ale when Ridley came upon them.

"Look what the cat dragged in," said Brother Aaron. Slightly balder than he was when Ridley last saw him, he nonetheless had retained the same youthful glint in his light brown eyes. He embraced Ridley, kissing him on the cheek.

The rest of the monks rose, each in turn greeting Ridley with similar affection.

"Don't let me interrupt," said Ridley.

"We were just having a friendly discussion about the Bible until His Holiness shows up with our orders," said Brother Hendrik, who gave a rather noisy stretch, revealing the massive, bodybuilder physique normally concealed beneath his robes.

"The story of the spikenard," said Brother Zigfried, lowering his head so that he stared at Ridley through the tops of his stony eyes. "Have you heard of it?"

"Heard of spikenard?" said Ridley. "Yeah, it was an expensive ointment used centuries ago."

"The biblical story itself, I mean," said Brother Zigfried, his words colored by his Oxford accent. "You see, the story goes that Mary, the sister of Martha, had cracked open a jar of the stuff and was using it to soothe Our Lord's poor feet. Well, Judas Iscariot, that jackanapes, says to Him, and I'm paraphrasing here, of course, 'Lord, you seem to be rather mindful of the poor, eh? What gives with the expensive lotion? It seems that we could have sold it and given the money to the poor, what do you say to that?' And Our Lord tells Judas that Mary will keep the ointment for His burial. 'For the poor always ye have with you,' He says, 'but me ye have not always.'"

"It's the wrong interpretation," said Brother Aaron, draining the last drop of ale from his glass.

"What do you mean?" Ridley asked.

"It makes Jesus sound, you know, whiny. Just give me this one little luxury, Judas, and get off my back. I'm convinced that something was lost in translation."

"He's saying, 'why not?'" said Brother Fernando. "So many poor people on earth, you can't possibly take care of them all at once. But that doesn't mean you can't try, which means that you have an obligation to preserve yourself for the task."

"No, but it just doesn't make any sense," said Brother Aaron. "Woe is me, I'm dying soon? That's preserving yourself for the task of healing the world?"

"It was a metaphor."

"Bull!" said Brother Aaron.

"I have to agree," said Ridley. "I would never call myself an expert, but in my opinion, the story is meant to illustrate that

Christ—or the philosophy He espoused—will always be with us, but only if we focus on what truly is important rather than what we *think* is important."

The monks fell silent, save for a gaseous rumble from Brother Hendrik's esophagus.

"Bull!" said Brother Aaron.

"Well," said Pope Leo, entering into the enclave. "Looks like we're in the midst of another debate."

At his entrance, Ridley and the Brothers rose.

"Sit down, sit down. Your beer will get warm. So what was it this time? First Corinthians?"

"Spikenard," said Brother Zigfried.

"Ah yes," said the pope. "A perennial favorite. But we have more pressing matters. Ridley is here on behalf of President Zimmer, because it has been agreed that I am to send you fine Brothers on another assignment."

The Brothers stiffened in rapt attention.

"A certain letter is rumored to have been found," he began. "It is known as the Nicene Cipher. Its author is rumored to be Simon Magus, a heretic who was a contemporary of Saints Peter and Paul. In it, Simon Magus alludes to a theory of Christ's divinity. He goes on to imply that St. Paul agreed with this theory. Subsequently, the letter was obtained by Marcion of Sinope, added to, and encrypted. In that cipher is a document that, but for an act of severe suppression by the early Church, could very well have been the foundation for an entirely new Christian-based faith."

Ridley found himself on the literal edge of his seat. He shuffled back self-consciously.

Brother Zigfried cleared his throat. "What is the nature of this... *testament?*"

"Be careful with your choice of phrasing," the pope said with a touch of annoyance. "Your job is going to be to ensure that *testament* does not turn out to be an accurate term. The nature, as you put it, is this: Marcion, using information from this letter, and with a careful reading of St. Paul's epistles, put forward a theory. The God of the Old Testament, he had concluded, seemed to have very different attributes from the God that Jesus spoke of in the New Testament. Marcion concluded that the God of the Old Testament, Yahweh the creator, was a lesser being, a petty, jealous being who had enslaved the human race. Jesus, Marcion said, was the son of a more powerful god, who offered his son as ransom for the human race. Those who followed this new god were to be freed; or, to put it in no uncertain terms, *saved*."

"Well," said Brother Hendrik, "I guess our work here is done. Nice knowing all of you."

"This is no time for jokes," Pope Leo said sternly. "The First Council of Nicaea put an end to what eventually became known as the Gnostic heresy. Hence the phraseology of the Nicene Creed: 'We believe in *one* God... Jesus Christ, the Son of God... *begotten, not made... being of one substance with the Father.*' These powerful words were chosen carefully, designed to carve the truth into stone. Marcion's ideas were suppressed, and Marcion himself driven out. The cipher changed hands several times after Marcion died, and always with the utmost secrecy. Heretics planned to one day use it as supposed evidence that the Catholic Church was founded on a lie. They could therefore overthrow the Church once and for all. Eventually, with no place else to hide the document in Constantine's Empire, a group of Marcionite heretics secreted the letter back to its place of origin, Nicaea, what is now modern day Iznik, and there they buried it beneath the niche of the Green Mosque in Bursa."

"The mosque was recently desecrated," added Ridley. "Those involved have been murdered."

"We think," said the pope, "that whoever is ultimately responsible for these murders, including that of my cousin, has possession of the Nicene Cipher. References have been made to removing the head, literally and figuratively."

No further explanation was necessary. The pope's tone was enough when he said, "You, brothers, are to find out who has the means to destroy the Catholic Church."

## ROME, ITALY

Ridley Shane tossed his suitcase on the bed and sat down next to it. He didn't feel like putting away his things right now. A shower, a shave, a good dinner—precisely in that order.

He had listened to the pope's story about the Nicene Cipher with the unwavering focus that his job demanded of him. Now, something nagged deep in his subconscious, a tiny voice he'd listened to before. Late afternoon was losing its hold on the day. Night was coming.

Fatigue weighed his limbs and stung his eyes when he blinked. At last he collapsed with his head landing in the center of the mushy motel pillow...

AND WAS in a very large theater. Every inch of the place was draped in black. He looked up at the balcony area and its alcoves where one could retreat and draw the curtains for privacy. He was standing on stage. Everywhere he looked, he just missed the flash of a curtain closing, and barely caught a glimpse of someone he'd known in his life. Cal Stokes, his new friend, the Marine's Marine, was up there. As Cal pulled the curtain closed, Ridley caught the scornful look on his friend's face.

In another alcove was Cal's best friend, in some ways Ridley's spiritual advisor, Daniel Briggs, the famed Marine sniper. The ethereal Marine gazed at him disapprovingly before pulling the curtain closed himself. It was the same with the others. Gaucho, Willie Trent, even Brandon Zimmer. All looked down on him, and all closed the curtain.

They were in there, hiding, their secrets thinly veiled from him. Their *sins*.

Suddenly, he got the sensation that he wasn't able to leave the stage. He could only remain there, alone as a dying insect, and feel the degradation of his comrades-in-arms. He heard demonic laughter, like the croaking of a toad, coming from behind the curtains.

He was rooted to the stage while the curtains rustled.

All around him, sin and depravity were having their way with the souls of his friends. It chewed at them until they were nothing but pulp.

A burst of mortar fire demolished half the stage.

A child's body lay next to him, legless.

Ridley Shane awoke, drenched in sweat, panting. It was something both familiar and unwelcome in Ridley's ordered world. Thank God for the sterile familiarity of a cheap motel.

He dialed the number he had been waiting to use.

"Hello, Ridley," said Brother Gabriel.

Ridley couldn't wait that long.

"I'm in Rome."

"Then be sure to do what the Romans do."

Ridley smiled at his friend's quip. It wasn't that funny, but it was pure Brother Gabriel. "I would if I could," he said. "I can't seem to feel like I'm in the right place."

"Forgive me, Ridley, but if I know you, I'd say it's possible you've never felt as if you were in the right place. You should give Haiti a try. Brother Luca and I have been here for a week and I still can't get used to the food."

"Haiti, huh? Do I want to know?"

"Fact-finding mission."

"Ah."

There was an awkward pause, as Ridley fought for the words.

"So," said Brother Gabriel. "How are... things?"

"You've been briefed on why I'm here?"

"His Eminence sent me the file this afternoon."

"Then you know..."

"Know what?"

"How... *dire* it is."

There was a pause on the other end, then, "What's troubling you, Ridley?"

"The darkness," he said plainly.

"The darkness."

"Listen, I've been in battle. I've seen the worst that humanity has to offer. But I've also seen the best of mankind. I can't wrap my head around what I'm feeling. This split between good and evil. For the first time in a long time, I'm... uneasy. Like I've taken a wrong step and can't turn back."

Brother Gabriel laughed. "I have a pretty good idea what's ailing you, friend."

"And what's that?"

"You're human, Ridley. I think you forget that at times. Get some rest. We'll see you next week."

"Thanks, I got some rest. I think I'll go for a walk."

"Hang in there, friend. I will see you soon."

"Thanks."

He hung up feeling as if Brother Gabriel had somehow transported through the phone and materialized in spirit next to him.

Ridley was left with a lingering sense of calm. It was the power that all the Brothers possessed, this ability to inspire awe and confidence in Ridley Shane. Not an easy task, considering what the covert agent had seen and done in his life.

He got up, showered, shaved, and left the motel.

# TILLINGS NECK, NY

Forty-two hundred miles away, a kid named Scott Hampton found a nickel. Heads up. Good luck.

One problem. His dad had recently told him that picking up coins that were heads up was superstitious, and that was bad. But Scott Hampton was thirteen. Thirteen is the age where boys tread on the cusp between the silky innocence of their childhood and the stone-cut sharpness of adult responsibility. And somewhere between those two points is the shadow where naive dreams gasp their last breath.

He wanted that nickel. It was heads up. Yes, it was superstitious. Yes, it was stupid. But he had to pick it up.

He'd just come from the Tillings Neck library. Laurie Martin was there. She had freckles between her eyes, and when she smiled it was like it had been made for him. But today she was with some other kid—Joe? Jim? Whatever—and he was all sliding up to her and she laughed and she smiled the smile that had been made only for Scott Hampton. Now that smile was being poured into a strange vessel.

Rather than ride his bike home, he opted instead to push it. He wanted to physically feel the burn of rejection.

Eyes to the ground, dejected, he saw the nickel. Heads up. If he didn't pick it up, he'd never know whether his luck might turn or not. He bent down.

There was a sharp pop in the distance, and something zipped over his head.

Instinctively, he picked his head up. Three more pops. And then a scream that he would never forget, full of terror.

Scott Hampton got on his bike and pedaled as if the devil was on his tail. He looked into his side mirrors and saw his own panicked face there. He pedaled harder.

A black sedan sped toward him. He swerved to the side of the road, nearly dumping into the drainage ditch. The car screeched to a halt.

The driver got out. He was bleeding from the mouth.

He looked at Scott. "Would you please call a doctor?" the man said. He wilted, and then collapsed like a marionette with broken strings.

Scott Hampton went up to the guy tentatively. He touched the guy's neck like they did on CSI. Scott's hand came away dark with blood.

---

SCOTT WAS white when his mother found him. He didn't remember any of the details later when she retold the story of how he came in, a bloody stain across his shirt like he'd been splashed from a thick brush of brick red paint.

But he remembered the look of horror on her face. And her words, so calm, so collected, so numbed with abject horror that it terrified him: "Is that blood?" He answered her with an affirmative nod. "Is it yours?"

He broke down in her arms. His mother called the police.

## TILLINGS NECK, NY

"We got another one," said Detective Little, poking his head into his chief's office.

"You're kidding," said Maddox. "Where?"

"Two miles from the Dempsey house. A kid found him. Said the guy came out of his car and collapsed. He'd been shot."

"Shit. Tell me he's still got his head."

"He does."

"You sure it's related?"

"No."

Maddox paused. "I'm confused. Why did you say it was *another one?*"

"Because of the book they found in his car."

"Back up. What book?"

Little entered fully into Maddox's office and placed a series of photos in front of him. "Look at the title."

Maddox squinted as he read: "*Marcion and the Heretics, a Speculative Study.* Is that supposed to mean something to me?"

"Look at this one," he said, handing over another photo.

"*The Catholic Church and its Enemies.* Again, is this something that I should be getting?"

"One more."

He squinted at the book in the third photo. "*The Nicene Cipher: How a Legendary Text Could Destroy the Catholic Church.*" He looked up at Little, whose Irish eyes beamed at him. "OK, so?"

"Chief, every one of these books is railing against the Church. Even this one, this Marcion thing. It's all about Christian heresy. We got a dead priest, and then this guy shows up dead with anti-Christian paraphernalia in his possession."

"I'm not seeing it. You can't bust a guy over what's in his library. My wife's got a copy of *Mein Kampf* on the shelf at home that she used to teach in her AP History class. Sorry, get some harder evidence."

"Chief," he said.

"What?"

"We had a look at his search history. He was researching Tom Dempsey."

Maddox sat back in his chair. "Alright now. Anyone talking?"

"A woman saw him outside his car taking pictures of St. Matthew's Church on Canal Street with his cell phone. A red SUV drives by slowly and shoots four times without stopping. Three of them hit the target. The woman screams, and the victim, name of Jofar Aslan, stumbles away and gets in his car. Drives for about a block and nearly runs down the kid who spots him. Aslan stops, gets out, dies."

Maddox ran the scenario over in his head. "OK, put out an APB for a red SUV. I'm guessing she didn't get a plate."

"No, sir."

"Of course not. Why should she make our lives easier?"

"One more thing."

Maddox put his head in his hands. "God, what now?"

"Listen, Chief—"

"My wife's been texting me nonstop since I left the house this morning. She's three days past her due date and we're out of Doritos. Forgive me if I'm a little tense here."

"I'll come back."

"No, no," said Maddox, a modicum of guilt seeping into his conscience. "What'd you have to tell me?"

"An item appeared in the New York Post this morning. I never read it. The headline popped up in my Facebook feed. Pope Leo has been notified of the death of his cousin, our Father Norman."

"Any comments from the pope?"

"Your standard 'asking for prayers' statement issued from the Vatican. That's all. They're keeping a distance."

"OK. Keep me up to date."

Little left his office. Maddox opened his top desk drawer and pulled out a bottle of Mylanta. He gave it a shake and took a chalky swig.

He was beginning to regret waking up this morning.

# ROME, ITALY

T he aroma here was intoxicating. The smell of freshly baked bread, of heavenly fried dough, fruity olive oil, and all manner of sweets lingered like a huge, benevolent hand having descended to sweep up the inhabitants of Via del Moro. It was a delicious place to be this time of day.

The cobblestone street was only slightly wider than a single car, and a compact one at that, and wound around tightly packed buildings.

The source of the lovely aroma was obvious: La Renella, a tiny bakery and pizzeria set into a building as if a space had been gouged out especially for it. Partially obscured by the only trees on the block, La Renella's arched entrance beckoned Ridley forward.

If the outside of the building smelled like the gateway to paradise, the inside was paradise itself. He sidled up to the glass case, which boasted all manner of baked goods, sweet and savory alike. A *mezzaluna*, the crescent-shaped cookie coated with powdered sugar caught his eye. He ordered a half a dozen along with a cup of black coffee and took it to a long bar counter set against the wall.

He took out his phone and was about to have a look at his email when, out of the corner of his eye, he became aware of someone staring at him. No stranger to confrontation, he looked directly at the person. A woman was seated at a small table at about eight o'clock from his position. She held up her cup of coffee in a small toast and smiled at him. She was brunette, with the olive skin of the region. She wore a black sun dress, and there was a floppy straw hat on the table before her.

Ridley gave a nod, no smile, and turned his attention to his cell phone. Just as his email feed refreshed itself, the woman was at his side. The floppy hat went down on the bar, and the woman perched upon the stool next to him.

"Their *mezzalunas* are world-renowned," she said with just enough of an accent to tie her to the area.

Ridley Shane had no time for women in his life at the moment. He didn't go out of his way to avoid the fair sex, but he preferred to impose a kind of distance – a psychic fence that projected through his skin – in order to let them know that he was off-limits. Those who didn't heed this projection were either dense or unwisely persistent. Either way, they needed to gear up for a cold shoulder that would leave them frostbitten.

So when she commented on his sweet snack, he nodded to her again, this time coupled with an unmistakably dismissive, "Thank you."

With his peripheral vision, he saw that she'd tilted her head and was staring at him. It was starting to get annoying.

"Daniel Briggs says 'hello'," she said.

He looked at her. Her face was beaming with an "I gotcha" smile.

He shook his head. "Come again?"

She leaned in. She smelled like rose water. "I said, Daniel Briggs says 'hello'. And the *mezzalunas* are world-renowned." She held out her hand. "I'm Beatricia Nespoli."

"I'm sorry, I thought you'd be—" he stopped himself short.

"A man?"

Ridley shrugged.

She looked around, as if to gauge who, if anyone, might be listening in, then lowered her voice. "You're working with others, I'm told."

He looked at her. It was obvious from her tone that her knowledge of the Brotherhood of St. Longinus ended with the generic word "others".

"I am," he said.

"Our mutual friend told me to offer you any guidance you might need."

Ridley sipped his coffee, not answering.

"You don't want my help."

"I didn't say that."

"Then what's on your mind, Ridley?"

He turned to her. "I don't know you."

The woman hesitated for the first time, like she was reshuffling the sales pitch in her head.

"Would it help if I told you what I know?"

"It might."

"Well," she said, nibbling her bottom lip, "I don't know *who* your operation involves, but as far as *what* it involves, I have some idea: holy war."

Those two words floated heavily in the tiny cafe.

"Keep going," he said.

"You're interested now," she said coyly.

"Intrigued. Not exactly the same thing."

"What we're talking about here is Gnostic holy war. Gnosticism postulates a duotheistic nature to the universe. Gnostics, as they're known, believe that there is the supreme god, which they call the 'monad', and a lesser, crueler god, whom they call the 'demiurge'. This demiurge was responsible for creating the material world. It's similar to the concept of God and the devil, although the differences between the two concepts are obvious."

"OK," he said. "But how does it tie in here?"

She ran a hand through her bob hairdo. "I've been briefed on the case you're working on. The murder of the student, Schell. He was the son of a U.S. senator, no?"

"Possibly."

"And he had found a certain map."

"Maybe."

"The map indicated the location of the Nicene Cipher."

He didn't know whether to be impressed or annoyed. The more people who knew about a secret...

"And so," she continued, "I can point you in the direction you need to go. I know... some things. Like who might be responsible for killing Mehmet Aslan and stealing the cipher."

"You know about that, too, then."

"I know all about this case, Ridley. I've been briefed well. For instance, did you know there have been murders in the States? Two men, one involved with Martin Schell, the other an innocent priest, someone at the wrong place at the wrong time, as you Americans are fond of saying. And then there was a third, a man by the name of Jofar Aslan."

Ridley didn't like how openly the woman threw around names in public. This conversation was better held in a private hotel room. But if she could help, why not let her carry on?

"And?"

"Jofar is Mehmet Aslan's brother. The two had joined with a religious cult called the Hand of Marcion. Now, normally, those relative few who espouse Gnostic philosophy aren't involved in anything sinister. You should understand that. This particular group is a fringe, a minority among the minority, but they are devout. And with devotion, as you know, Ridley, comes a relentless pursuit of the extreme."

He pursed his lips in deep thought for a moment, then asked, "What else do you know about the Hand of Marcion?"

"Not much else. They live in secrecy. I do know their leader is an American. I do not know his name. He is well insulated from the public eye."

Ridley brooded on this for a moment, when Beatricia's plaintive voice broke through.

"Use extreme caution, Ridley. I don't know much about this American, but I do know that he is a very dangerous man. What he says, his followers do without question. As you already know, they are not above murder. And their veins run far."

He stared at her earnest face.

"How do you know this?" he asked, suspecting that the answer held great weight.

She sat up straight and took a deep breath. "Mehmet Aslan was my boyfriend."

"That clears up the mystery a bit. How did he get involved with the cult?"

"He was dragged in by his brother, Jofar."

"Did he break up with you right away, or did he wait?"

She looked at him with narrow eyes. "You're very perceptive, Ridley."

"I know that cult members usually get touchy about dating outside the circle."

"Mehmet cut off all contact with me, then broke it off officially, all without so much as a single tear. There was a phone call: 'I am finished with unbelievers,' he said, and hung up."

"I have a feeling the story doesn't end there."

"You're correct. One day, about six months later, he called me out of the blue. His voice sounded terrible. Tight, and afraid. He said he wanted to get out of the cult. He acknowledged that it was indeed a cult, and that he didn't know how to get out of it. This was when news about the map discovery had leaked out among academics. He said Jofar was going to America to find the map, believing that it resided with the American who found it."

"Thomas Dempsey," said Ridley.

"That's the one. Mehmet said he had inside information that the map rested with one of Dempsey's students who was still in Turkey. Mehmet... retrieved the map from him."

"Retrieved? Interesting choice of words."

"I'm afraid he did it violently."

"Why was he so intent on 'retrieving' it?"

"He wanted to dig up the cipher and destroy it. He was certain it would lead to hellish religious conflict, the likes of which we have never seen in recent times."

She stopped talking and her face fell. She licked her lips before continuing. "I guess he found what he was looking for."

"And then someone found him," said Ridley.

## ROME, ITALY

Beatricia Nespoli left the cafe, pulling on her floppy straw hat and sliding a pair of Greta Garbo sunglasses onto her face before exiting through the back. Ridley sat and finished his coffee, thinking intensely. He wanted to put a face on this nemesis of the Church. To have the face be merely an opposing doctrine was disconcerting to say the least. How do you fight a doctrine?

He gathered himself and left the cafe, exiting out onto Via del Moro. The sun was setting, throwing long shadows onto the cobblestones. He made his way to the end of the street where it curved around to the backs of buildings. Not a soul to be found, like a deserted alleyway that stretched for the length of an entire block.

Suddenly a motorbike sputtered loudly and whirled around the corner. A well-dressed kid rode toward him. Ridley stepped aside. The kid eased off the accelerator as he approached. Then Ridley watched his arm go the side of the bike and pull out something that looked like a baton. The kid whirled it in the air, just as he passed Ridley.

The street was not wide enough, and the kid knew how to use the street. Ridley was backed up against a concrete wall.

The stick swung in an arc, and Ridley did the best he could: he balled himself up, ready to take the blow. The stick caught his shoulder blade. It stung, sending shocks through his entire body.

*The damn thing is electrified!* he thought, struggling to maintain his usual calm through the jolt.

He stood up, dazed, his body tingling. The bike took a skidding turn, came around again, the stick in the air. Impressively agile despite the cramped space, Ridley threw up a leg in a roundhouse kick when the rider returned. The kid parried it with his forearm, and Ridley was ready.

He struck quickly, grabbing the prod by the shaft and ramming it with all his might into the kid's ribs. He felt the telltale crack as the kid doubled over with a violent gasp. Ridley grabbed the baton and turned the business end on its owner. The kid went into a convulsive fit. Ridley let up. The kid was jittering like a fish.

Ridley tossed the prod aside, then picked the kid up by the lapels and threw his jellied body up against the wall.

With another convulsive jerk, the back of the kid's head slammed against the wall. He was out cold. Ridley eased his body to the ground.

A couple came around the corner, hand in hand. Ridley locked eyes with them. The girl put one hand to her mouth and pointed with the other.

This was no time to conjure up excuses in broken Italian. He turned and ran as fast as he could in the opposite direction, grabbing the cattle prod along the way.

# VATICAN CITY

"We need to talk."

"I was wondering when you'd call," said Daniel Briggs.

Ridley sat in his tiny motel room, nursing his bruised shoulder with an ice pack. He decided he'd had worse.

"I just had a couple of interesting run-ins," said Ridley. "One nice, one not so nice."

"You OK?"

"Yeah, maybe. I don't know. Zimmer brief you on this?"

"I heard some things," answered Daniel vaguely.

"You know about this girl, Nespoli?"

"*Doctor* Nespoli. She holds a PhD in Comparative Religion, with a specialty in Gnosticism. I guess Brandon thought you might like a little more scholarly guidance on this one. It's an unusual case despite your background."

"I suppose it wouldn't do any good right now to remind you how much I hate surprises."

"Don't take it personally, Ridley. The man was just trying to help."

"Help is fine. I would have liked a heads-up."

"Chalk it up to poor judgment," said Daniel. "He's a Democrat, remember?"

They both laughed.

"Is this line safe?" Ridley asked, the suspicion finally creeping into his voice.

"We're fine. *No one* can hear us."

"Same one the president uses?"

"The very same," said Daniel. "Ridley, what's wrong?"

"Well, it's just that *someone* knew I was there besides her."

There was a pause on the line. "Your other run-in?"

"Guy on a motorbike. Had a cattle prod on him."

Daniel sighed, barely audible. "Do you have a description? I could get our friends in the Italian police after him."

"Tell them to look for a kid with a concussion, a couple of broken ribs, and a newly-formed fear of electricity. I have his cattle prod here. I might be able to get some prints off of it. I'll let you know if I need any further help. I'd like to keep this thing out of anyone else's hands."

"Good choice," said Daniel.

RIDLEY MADE his way back to the Papal Palace, turning the events of the day around in his head. If his communications with President Zimmer were secure, and all communications from Daniel and The Jefferson Group, Ridley's current employer, were just as secure, then the only other answer was that someone here was a mole.

But that was absurd. Who could it be? The pope? The Brothers? No way.

He arrived back at the palace in time to visit with Pope Leo before evening prayers. The pope was walking through his private garden, hands clasped behind his back, lost in thought. When he saw Ridley, he started. Ridley must have looked more disheveled than he thought.

"My goodness," the pope exclaimed.

Ridley thought, *You should see the other guy*, but held his tongue out of reverence. "I'm OK, Your Eminence."

The pope looked about, then pointed to a young man bent over a plot of land near the edge the garden. "You," he said in Italian, "why are you planting at this hour? Get up and get some medical help for Mr. Shane."

The young man looked up, his face a mask of shame and contrition. He ran into the palace like his life depended on it.

"I am sorry," he said to Ridley. "You know I do not normally lose my temper. It has been a long day, and we have had some turnover within the grounds staff. They are still learning. Sit down, my friend."

Ridley sat down, feeling the burn of the day's activity in his joints.

"Easy, my friend," said Pope Leo. "You won't always have your youth. Take care of your body. Now, your face and clothing tell me you have something to discuss. But first, where is that young man?"

"What young man?"

"The one I sent to fetch you some aid. You can't trust these—"

"Excuse me," said Ridley, not caring one bit about interrupting His Holiness mid-sentence, "did you say he was new?"

"I did."

Ridley looked over to where the young man had been standing. Looked toward the palace. Looked back again.

If his Italian was any good, he had heard Pope Leo chastise the man for planting at this hour. But where the man had been standing was nothing but an unused area at the end of the garden next to a large marble vase. The turf next to the vase had been dug up and replaced haphazardly, not neatly overturned like a garden.

There was a flash of light.

The explosion ripped through the air just as Ridley dove into the pope's body and the two men went flying to the ground.

# VATICAN CITY

The Vatican security team was quick to arrive, along with the Swiss guard from the papal apartments. The smoke had yet to clear before the Brothers of St. Longinus had converged at the site.

They helped Ridley and the pope to their feet.

"Your Holiness," said Brother Hendrik, lifting the man up as if he weighed no more than a toddler.

The pope held up a hand and murmured in Italian, "I am not hurt."

Ridley, helped to his feet by Brother Fernando, got his bearings, steadying himself on the short but sturdy monk.

"God is watching you," said Brother Zigfried. "Look at the shrapnel." He pointed to the veranda, which had been riddled with a spray of metal.

The pope took a steadying breath and patted Ridley on the arm. "Thank you, my friend."

Ridley nodded reverently.

"I think I should lie down," the pope said, gladly accepting Brother Aaron's firm grip.

Ridley and the Brothers escorted the pope back toward the palace.

"The worker out there before," said Ridley, rubbing where his elbow had collided with the ground. "Anyone see him?"

"What worker?" asked Brother Fernando.

"I'm a fool," said the pope.

"You can't read minds, Your Holiness," said Ridley.

"You did," the pope returned.

"By the grace of God," said Brother Zigfried.

"I think we can all agree that this place could use a little extra security," said Brother Aaron.

"I concur," said Ridley. "I don't know how that guy got in, but I know we can't trust any new faces around here."

───────

IT WAS EARLY the next morning, and Ridley, hydrated and ibuprofen-eased, was touring the site of the previous night's near catastrophe with Brothers Luca and Gabriel, who had returned from Haiti that morning.

"Looks like he hid most of the components in this," Ridley said, pointing to the shattered remains of the marble vase at the edge of the garden. "My guess is that it was modular. He probably had been sneaking components in bit by bit. Last night, it was just a matter of assembling it quickly."

His cell phone rang. The caller ID read DANIEL BRIGGS. Ridley answered the call. "We're alive."

"Thank God for that."

"Yeah, there's a lot of that going around here."

"No one seriously hurt?"

"I got a bum leg out of the deal. Other than that, and a few bruises from a little brawl yesterday, I'm fine."

"How's His Holiness?"

"His Holiness is resilient, I have to say."

"And the security situation?"

"Better now that Brother Luca and Brother Gabriel are here to help fortify the ranks. We're not letting any strangers in. The Swiss Guard is on max alert."

"What about the culprit?"

"The authorities are putting a trace on him. His Holiness gave a good description, and I added what I could. We have a name too, but we're ninety nine percent sure it's an alias."

"What's the name?"

"He's registered here as 'Bruce Banner'."

"You're kidding."

"Nope."

"The Hulk?"

"Yep."

Ridley thought he heard Daniel grunt over the line. "And no one caught it?"

"They're not big into comics here."

There was a sigh on the other end. "Sure you don't need anything?"

"Only the location of the bad guys."

"I would tell you if I could," Daniel answered.

Ridley hung up the call and turned to the Brothers. "Let's have a look at the security footage."

# VATICAN CITY

Brother Aaron bowed to the pope. "Your Eminence, we have footage of the man who planted the bomb."

"And I see you are about to embark on a mission," returned His Holiness, noting the monk's plain clothes.

"Yes, these," said Brother Aaron, feeling suddenly self-conscious in the Pope's office, as if he were standing there naked. "Forgive me. We'll need to blend in."

"Of course," the pope said, bowing his head in an approving nod.

"If I may, Your Eminence," said Brother Aaron, approaching the desk with a computer tablet turned forward. "You can see here the man identified as 'Bruce Banner'," he paused to note a disapproving glance from the pope, who had been briefed earlier on the trivial significance of the name. The suspect's alias was an embarrassing joke that the Brothers were becoming ever more reluctant to bring up. "As I was saying, the man is seen here moments after planting the bomb. He is leaving the palace here..." He swiped the screen to reveal a frozen image of the man on his way out of the building. "And here we see him entering a vehicle. We were able to zoom in and increase resolution on the image to reveal a plate number. We are at the moment retrieving the identity of the vehicle's owner."

The pope breathed a heavy sigh. "Is that all?"

Brother Aaron's mouth went dry. Pope Leo was seldom unapproachable. His awe of the man increased tenfold, he found, when the pope was brooding and under duress.

"That is all, Your Eminence."

"I would like to see the man brought to justice."

"Of course," Brother Aaron said reverently.

The pope stared at him intently. "You must fully understand the implications of what I am saying."

"Yes, Your Eminence."

"He is to be brought to justice, even though I have already forgiven him."

Brother Aaron bowed his head respectfully. The pope was a complex man, and his complexity was showing now in his brooding avoidance of feelings of retribution. Justice and retribution were two different things, and there were few people in the world who understood the concept as well as the robed figure at the desk before him; though he was human, and had a spiritual struggle over the present matter. It was all the more reason Brother Aaron wanted to get this meeting over and done with.

"I understand, Your Eminence."

"God bless and keep you," Pope Leo said softly, a hand raised in blessing.

---

"THE OWNER IS A WHAT?" said Brother Fernando, examining his layperson's clothing in the mirror of his cell, his robe draped over his arm.

"A grocery store owner from Rome," said Brother Aaron,

reading off the printout of the report. A special program with direct access to the Rome Police Department's database had supplied the details; Brother Zigfried had provided the technical know-how to run a comprehensive search. It wasn't easy, and special precautions had to be undertaken. The Rome Police Department had no idea that their servers were being accessed in this manner.

"Antonio Fortini," continued Brother Aaron. "He owns a chain of grocery stores across Italy. We have his home address."

"Then what are we waiting for?"

"Waiting for the go-ahead from you."

Brother Fernando tossed his robe on his bed. "Let's go pay a visit to Signor Fortini."

They raced out of the apartments, each with his mind focused on the task before them. They were prepared for conflict, even though every precaution would be taken to ensure that no lives would be lost in the process of apprehending the elusive 'Mr. Banner.'

The house was a simple country style villa on Via del Borghese. Done in Spanish architecture, it was situated on a hill, separated from the road by a distance too far to walk.

"I don't like the looks of this," said Brother Fernando, as the car rolled carefully down a single-lane path that led to the villa. "If they've got cameras, they'll know we're here."

"And what if they do?" said Brother Aaron. "We're here on a photojournalism tour of Italy and we made a wrong turn."

"I told you I wasn't crazy about that story." Indeed, the two men had argued for the first quarter of their journey on the plausibility of the alibi; for one thing, neither man held a camera.

"I'll do the talking if it bothers you so much," said Brother Aaron, pulling off the path down a long, narrow driveway. He shut the car and looked at his companion. "Ready?"

"Let's do it."

They approached the house carefully, each man doing his best to do a surreptitious scan of the place for cameras, or inhabitants —for there were no cars anywhere.

"The house looks deserted," said Brother Fernando. The quiet did nothing to quell his suspicion that they were headed straight into an ambush.

They stepped up through the portico onto the shaded porch and knocked on the door. There was no bell.

No answer.

Brother Aaron knocked again. "Hello?"

It was quiet. So quiet that both the men found that they'd purposely slowed their breathing in order to focus on whatever sound might come from within.

A thump. The two men looked at each other.

Brother Aaron knocked again. "Hello? Signor Fortini?"

Brother Fernando shot him a stupefied look, which caused Brother Aaron to realize his mistake. If they were tourists who had gotten lost, how would they possibly know the name of the homeowner?

Brother Aaron's mind raced for a quick excuse. *Just wing it*, he thought.

He instinctively felt for the pistol in the holster behind his back, having the strange combination of safety and foreboding that comes with possessing a firearm in such a situation.

He knocked again. "Signor Fortini?"

Another thump from within.

Brother Fernando motioned for him to keep knocking and calling while he himself went sneaking around the side of the house. Stealthily approaching a side window, he moved slowly, hunched down below the level of the sill. Hugging the wall of the house, he poked his head up. In the distance, he heard Brother Aaron knocking and calling out. And here, through the window, he saw a man within, creeping toward the front door with a rifle in his hands.

Brother Fernando's adrenaline kicked in at that moment, and all the instincts of a fully-trained warrior clicked into gear. He drew his gun, and with the butt, hit the window as hard as he could. The window cracked in a splendid spider web, and between the spokes, Brother Fernando saw the man turn and point the rifle his way.

He ducked, just as the window exploded over him. He watched the glass rain on the ground.

BROTHER AARON HEARD the crack against the window, and was just wondering what his friend was doing on the side of the house, when a blast of gunfire and shattering glass rang out.

With his gun drawn, he backed up and rammed the door with his shoulder. He kicked the door several times, then rammed it again. It burst open.

He spilled into the house just in time to see Brother Fernando poised at the side window in a shooter's stance.

And just in time to see a man fleeing into the recesses of the house.

Brother Fernando leapt into the room. They took positions on either side of the threshold leading to the back hallway.

A door slammed shut deeper inside the home. Both men peeked down the narrow hallway, noticing several opened doors that lined it, and one closed one. Quickly padding over to the closed door, they took positions on either side.

"Come out," yelled Brother Aaron. "Whoever you are, we mean you no harm."

There was silence within.

Brother Aaron stiffened, not knowing whether he was ready to play door buster again.

He kicked with all his might, grunting gutturally as he did. The door fell in.

The homeowner lay on the floor, the gun at his side. His body was convulsing. They ran to his side. Brother Fernando kicked the rifle out of the man's reach while Brother Aaron reached into his mouth and grabbed his tongue.

The man stopped convulsing, a final breath escaping from his chest.

Brother Fernando kneeled down next to the body and put his fingers to the man's neck. He then motioned for Aaron to get out of the way and put his head close to the dead man's mouth. He sniffed, then looked up at Brother Aaron.

"Smells like almonds. Could be cyanide."

"Talk about a suicide bomber," said Brother Aaron.

Beatricia Nespoli entered the plant like a mouse among alley cats. Burly men moved huge, coarsely-carved cow carcasses on hooks across the room, the hind legs attached to ball bearing tracks on the ceiling. The place stunk like an open grave. A foreman shouted obscenities to the men to move faster, watch their steps, and went so far as to insult their mothers and sisters in the process.

She walked casually through, noting the way she, a reasonably attractive woman—if she did say so herself—could garner not a single eye from any of these men, so trained they were to ignore all things that were not part of their job.

"Excuse me," she said to the foreman, "I'm looking for Phillipo Martoni."

The foreman looked at her like she was a beef carcass that had gotten loose and dressed itself like a woman in order to escape.

"Excuse me," she repeated.

"I heard you, silly woman. He's in the office."

Beatricia made her way to the back of the plant where there was a staircase against the wall leading up to a wooden door. She knocked once, then opened it.

She found herself in a dark office. As her eyes adjusted to the dark, she realized that there was a single lamp upon a desk, lit with a low-wattage bulb.

A figure seated at the desk moved slightly and said, "You're early. I don't like it when people are early."

"I don't like it when people kill my boyfriend, but you don't hear me whining about it."

She heard a chuckle from behind the desk. Then the man stood up and came around.

He was a young man, aged by violence. His face was pock-marked and hard, and the eyes, sunken into the face and hooded by a thick brow, were stony and devoid of life.

"Where's the big man?" she said.

"I'm helping you now, Beatricia."

She hated the way he said her name, like it stuck to the roof of his mouth.

"Your boss won't like it."

"I told you on the phone, he's out on business."

"What kind of business?"

"None of your concern, Beatricia."

"Who killed Mehmet?" she asked, ready to be gone from the foul place.

The man spread his arms. "No hug first?"

"Don't give me that crap."

"You know, I remember when Mehmet would talk about you. He said you were, pardon me, wonderful in the sack."

"Screw you."

An oily smile appeared on the man's face. "I knew I would like you. Mehmet used to show me pictures."

"Who killed him?"

"Beatricia, would you like to know why I scheduled this meeting when the Leader was away?"

She had to remind herself to keep cool. "It did cross my mind."

"You were prepared to offer him something, were you not? Money? Something?"

She hesitated before answering. "I was."

"And do you think he would have given you the name of Mehmet's killer so easily? For a mere cash payment?"

"I figured a guy like that has to have a price. We all do."

"Yes, we all do. The Leader, however, is a much more devoted man that you give him credit for. He doesn't want money. He wants loyalty. He wants devotion. He wants... a soldier for the cause."

"So, all I have to do is pledge allegiance to your filthy cult and I get all the answers I want."

"That's no way to talk. I don't insult *your* Church with its twisted doctrine and bizarre rituals, do I? And no, you wouldn't get the answers you desire, because they wouldn't matter. They don't matter. All that matters is what the Leader wishes to see come to fruition."

"And that is?"

"I think you know."

"You'll never get away with it."

"Let us worry about that."

Her mouth had gone dry. She tried in vain to salivate, moving her tongue around, and producing terrible, nervous clicking sounds in the process.

It seemed to amuse the man. "You are adorable, Beatricia. Much prettier than those pictures that Mehmet used to show me. Tell me, are there more? Were there... boudoir photos?"

"Enough already."

"Are you getting uncomfortable?"

"Worse. I'm getting angry."

The man pouted his lips in mockery. "Tch tch tch, I'm terribly sorry. Well then, let's talk business. The Leader, as I've said, does not have a price. But I do. Give me what I want, and you will have the name of Mehmet's killer. It's that simple."

"Really," she said incredulously.

"I want what you were going to give the Leader."

"That's all?"

"That's all."

"You don't expect me to carry that kind of money around with me wherever I go, do you? I was going to suggest a dead drop."

"Very well, a dead drop."

He smiled lasciviously. It made her skin crawl. But somehow, her loathing gave her strength. She thought of Mehmet, the man he was before he had been drained of his soul by these people. She remembered the desperation in his voice when she spoke with him for the last time. They hadn't taken all of his soul.

"So," she said, "how do we do this?"

He walked past her to the door. He clicked the lock shut. Then he turned, undoing his belt buckle. "First, you get on your knees."

A wave of revulsion nearly overcame her. She walked toward him. She was inches from his face. "I don't want to do this."

"*Bambina*," he cooed, "give me what I want, and you will have whatever you ask."

She looked him up and down. He was grotesque. She slowly went to her knees...

And grabbed him like she was crushing a piece of foil.

He yowled once and quickly lost his breath in a pinched whine. Then Beatricia Nespoli stood up and head-butted the man in the face, sending him reeling back against the door.

Blood spewed from his nose like a broken water pipe. One of his hands clutched at his groin, the other at his face. He whined like a child and curled to the floor.

She fixed her hair, stepped past him, and unlocked the door.

His friends would have known him as Cyrus Knox. If he had any friends. He had only disciples. And so he was known as the Leader.

The Leader stood over the seated figure of Martoni, who had removed the ice pack from his face when he entered. Martoni was buttressed on either side by two disciples. Each put a hand on his shoulder when Knox entered.

"You got your ass kicked by a woman," he said.

The disciple on Martoni's left let out a snorting chuckle, to which Knox shot a look of reproach. The man stifled his laughter.

"Have you anything to say?"

"No, Dear Leader," said Martoni.

"How did this happen?" asked Knox, pulling up a chair and sitting neatly in front of the man.

Martoni licked his lips. "I was sitting here going over the books when she came in to see me. She was furious, screaming and ranting. 'Who killed my boyfriend? Who was it? I demand to know!' and so on. I told her to go to hell. That's when she attacked me."

"Attacked you?" asked the Leader.

"I had risen from the desk to call security. She put her hands on me. She had totally changed. She was caressing me... down there... and she all of a sudden head-butted me in the face."

Knox smiled. He patted Martoni's knee like a doting father. Then he grabbed Martoni's nose between his first two fingers.

Martoni let out a sound that wasn't human.

Knox let go of the nose, shoving the head back in the process. Immediately the ice pack came up. One of the disciples grabbed it from his hands and chucked it across the room.

"You idiot!" howled Knox, rising from his seat. The rage in him had built to a holy fire. "We have this entire place bugged! I've seen the video and listened to your despicable behavior!"

Martoni's face was a mask of pure horror. "Dear Leader," he wailed, "forgive me! I am a weak man! Forgive me!"

Knox walked over and put a gentle hand on the man's head, which was bowed as the man wept bitterly.

---

ALONE, he contemplated the document before him, sealed within the glass hermetic case. Soon, he would have possession of the means to decipher it: the gold scepter of Mithridates IV, ruler of the Parthian dynasty. He closed his eyes, picturing the simplistic beauty of the scepter in his hands, shining in the light of the sun. He could feel it. It was within his grasp. He would have it soon. And soon, his holy war would begin.

He caressed the top of the smooth glass leaving a smear of grease atop it. He put his face up to it and exhaled, watching the patch of fog widen and then thin away to nothing.

There was a knock at his office door.

"Come in."

A disciple entered.

"Martoni has been prepared for stage two."

"Very well. You may proceed."

"He is weak."

Knox glared at the man. "Are you feeling sympathy for the traitor?"

"No, Dear Leader."

"Good, because I thought for a moment that you were implying that you were concerned for his safety."

"I was merely saying, Dear Leader, that he is in danger of..." He searched for the right word. "... expiring. If you wish to do with him what you indeed wish to do, he is going to need a period of rest. And allow me, Dear Leader, to say that I think it would be beneficial to pay him a kindness."

Cyrus Knox grinned at the man. "You are a loyal soldier, and you have a good head. Very well, I will pay him a visit. He likes chocolate, no? I'll bring him some chocolate. Then you may begin stage two of his conversion. Scourge him like Our Lord."

"Thank you, Dear Leader."

"And tell the others to prepare for a meeting after stage two is complete."

"Yes, Dear Leader."

---

THE MEETING CONSISTED of the highest ranks of the Hand of Marcion. Fifty-two men, no women. These men were the first inductees, the Chosen Few, as the Leader preferred to call them. They gathered in a rented hall on the outskirts of Sant'Antimo. A small fold-out conference table sat next to a hand-me-down podium.

When he entered to a fanfare of "We Shall Overcome" played on an MP3 player at ear-splitting level, they stood and erupted into thunderous applause.

He stepped to the podium and held up his hand. They quieted in unison.

"Friends, today is the darkest of days," he began. The place was completely silent now. "Within our ranks, the most diabolical of plots festers." A murmur escaped from one part of the audience. "Yes, today is a dark day. But we see the light of the Supreme, the Monad, coming through for us. His Son, Jesus, the manifestation of this light, has shown us the way toward true salvation. Let us pray now that we have the strength to ascend the summit of our destiny."

*"God, save us!"* came a shout from the audience.

"Yes, God save us all." He held up his hand and motioned to the disciple standing guard at the door.

Martoni entered, flanked by two disciples. He was not physically restrained, merely escorted, and that at a respectable distance. They moved to the side of the room while Martoni walked up to the podium. Cyrus Knox took a step aside, smiling like a man who'd waited an eternity for a best friend's entrance.

"Gentlemen," Martoni began in his non-voice as he extracted a piece of paper from his back pocket. "Forgive me, I fell while bike riding in Casoria and broke my nose. My voice is not very strong." He coughed twice and then read carefully from the paper. "I have news of an insidious virus that has festered among us. Like a cancer, it needs to be removed before it spreads." He coughed into his hand, pointedly avoiding the gaze of his audience. "The following men are guilty in a plot to overthrow our Dear Leader..." Here his voice broke away completely. He paused to wipe his tears on his sleeve.

Cyrus Knox wept and wiped his eyes as well.

"Will the following men please stand?"

There were murmurs in the crowd.

Martoni went on to read the names of ten men.

The atmosphere in the room became leaden yet electrified, as in the moments before a lightning storm. Men were weeping uncontrollably as the accused stood, then were forcefully led out of the room by disciples.

When Martoni was done, he said, "All hail our Dear Leader, for he is wise and just and loves us with his entire being."

The audience stood up and cheered wildly, enraptured, hands and heads in the air, wailing and crying ecstatically.

Cyrus Knox embraced Martoni, who gave no sign of emotion.

Knox took the podium, wiping his eyes, weeping outwardly and without shame. "Friends, you are my loyal followers. I love you like no other. Let us ascend to the light together! We shall upend the corrupt Church, the false Church, and we shall rule as was always our divine right to do so!"

The men cheered uncontrollably.

When they had settled down, they were led out of the hall. In the back, in the woods, ten graves had been dug. Ten men stood before them, sobbing, pleading for their lives through gagged lips.

The Leader stalked the remaining men, the loyal ones, searching their eyes. A disciple followed behind him carrying a laundry basket filled with ten pistols.

Cyrus Knox randomly chose ten executioners, who trembled and wept as they shot their brothers in the head, and watched as the bodies fell lifeless into the dark pits below.

## VATICAN CITY

Ridley hovered over Brother Zigfried's computer.

"Do you mind, ol' boy? I have an aversion to folks breathing over my shoulder."

Ridley stood up. He knew not to take any of the Brothers' good-natured jibing personally. It was like being back with Daniel and the TJG gang. The difference was the men in this room possessed an otherworldly quality that he couldn't quite describe. He knew one thing: whereas with The Jefferson Group he felt at home, here he felt like he was welcomed back from a long journey.

Brother Zigfried ran the scan of the fingerprints taken from the cattle prod. Once again, a hack into the Rome Police Department's database proved to be a small miracle in itself.

"Ah yes," said Brother Zigfried, "here we go. Tanner Knox. He's from America. Looks like... yes, here we go. From Illinois, it seems. Father is the owner of a chain of meat packaging plants in the Midwestern United States. Has a history of petty theft and vandalism. What young Tanner is doing here is anyone's guess. But it does seem like he's up to no good, wouldn't you agree?" He looked up at Ridley.

"I'd say so."

"What's next, *cowboy*?" Brother Zigfried was uncomfortably stiff with American slang.

"We should probably dig into young Tanner's current whereabouts. Something tells me he's on the trail of the Nicene Cipher."

"You think so? You're sure it wasn't just a wayward youth gone rogue?"

"Call it a hunch."

Brother Zigfried held up a finger. "Hang on. I have an idea." His fingers tapped wildly at the keyboard. "I'm doing a search on the family. The father, Cyrus Knox – being some business owner of high standing – ought to have some information out there. *Hell-ooo*."

He turned the screen to Ridley. It was an old newspaper headline. Ridley read it aloud: "*Disgraced Preacher to Begin Anew as Entrepreneur.*"

The article described the rise and fall of Cyrus Knox, formerly *Father* Cyrus Knox, a pastor from the Church of St. Stephen in the Roman Catholic diocese of Paneville County, Illinois.

"He was involved in a scandal," said Ridley, scanning the article.

"Yes," said Brother Zigfried. "Looks like he was paying Caesar his due, eh?"

Ridley looked at the monk. He knew he couldn't fully appreciate the Englishman's sense of irony.

The article detailed a scandal in which Father Cyrus Knox received inflated funds and exaggerated exemptions from the state in exchange for urging parishioners to vote for certain politicians. It was a scandal involving the entire governing body of Paneville. And Father Knox was at the center of it all. The article said that he was the mastermind and the orchestrator. He laundered the money through Mexican businesses in the name of his brother, a certain Jeroboam Knox, who was now deceased. There was a short blurb that said the brother had died under "unusual circumstances". The article did not explain further.

Once he'd served a light sentence of community service and was defrocked, the former Father Cyrus Knox reinvented himself as a minor king of the Midwest meat industry.

Brother Zigfried sat back in his chair. "Most interesting, wouldn't you say?"

"I would say."

"You think he's involved?"

"I don't know," said Ridley. "I do know that a kid like this may be free to make his own way in the world, but if he's involved in the family business..."

"Say no more," said Brother Zigfried, typing the name Cyrus Knox into his modified search engine.

An obscure website popped up. Ridley had to blink twice to make sure he was seeing it correctly.

The site was titled, "The Hand of Marcion."

The two men exchanged glances.

"Ol' boy, do you think we ought to call a meeting with the Brothers?"

"I think that's a good idea."

---

RIDLEY HAD some time before the meeting. Brothers Aaron and Fernando were off tracing the whereabouts of the saboteur known as Bruce Banner. And so he went back to his motel for a short rest.

And had the dream again.

There was the stage. And the balconies with their curtained alcoves. And his friends mocked him. The curtains closed and the screams fell on his ears. Demonic laughter. The trappings of evil deeds.

He saw one other figure he'd not seen in previous dreams. It was Beatricia Nespoli. She was alone in an alcove, staring at him accusingly. Her dark hair and olive skin stood in stark contrast to the snowy white dress she wore.

A stain appeared on her dress.

A black stain, like ink spreading on a damp paper towel. It started at her heart, and as she stared at him, it spread and covered her entire body. She dripped with it. And she grinned. And the grin was malevolent, a demon in flesh. And she shut the curtains on him. And there was the sound of croaking laughter from within.

The explosion ripped half the stage into splinters. The body of a legless child slid toward him.

---

HE CALLED DANIEL BRIGGS. The Marine was taking some time off in the Green Mountains of Vermont.

"You've got perfect timing," Daniel answered, his voice dripping with what sounded like sarcasm.

"Just calling to check up on *you* for a change. How's Vermont?"

"Snowy. Cold. Beautiful. Did you know you can buy maple syrup at the gas station?"

"No way."

"Yeah. Pretty cool, if you like maple syrup."

There was a pause.

"Hey, Rid," said the concerned voice on the other end of the line, "everything alright?"

"Just a little shook up. Can't seem to get my bearings on this one."

"Sorry. Wish I could be there with you. Doc Higgins has got

Cal on mandatory vacation time though. Thought I'd tag along."
Dr. Alvin Higgins was the resident shrink and master interrogator
of The Jefferson Group.

"No offense, but I'm glad you're not here."

"Thanks, I think?"

"No, really. Hey listen, you know I'm, well, spiritual, right?"

Daniel chuckled at the understatement. Daniel had often
described his friend Ridley Shane as one of the most spiritual
men on the Earth, next to, of course, himself, though their spiri-
tuality wasn't exactly the same.

"What the hell's so funny?"

"Nothing. Go on."

Ridley took a studied pause. "Something's bugging me about
this case. I've seen things, you know that."

"We all have."

"Yeah, well, I'm not afraid of dying."

"I know."

"I've stared it in the face."

"OK."

"So why is this case giving me the shakes?"

Daniel Briggs chuckled on the other end. "Ridley, there are
few people on earth who've been on the kind of spiritual roller
coaster that you have. But do yourself a favor."

"What's that?"

"Take away the rituals and the doctrine and all that stuff that
comes along with the Catholic mass. What do you have?" asked
Daniel.

"Jesus Christ."

"Exactly. Now, what would Jesus do?"

"Get himself killed."

Daniel didn't laugh. "Pray on this one, my friend."

"Yeah, I will. Anyway, enjoy the rest of your vacation."

"I'm just upset there's no maple syrup in the water fountains."

Ridley laughed. "We all have our crosses to bear, I guess."

"Take care."

He hung up, feeling tight in the gut after speaking with his friend. There was one, however, with whom he hadn't spoken with yet.

Ridley got down on his knees, his elbows resting on the bed.

"Lord," he muttered, "I'm not good enough with words to tell you about what's going on. But I know you know what's in my heart. I need you to show me the way. Show me that the light will outshine the dark."

His phone beeped. A text.

It was Brother Zigfried. Tanner Knox had been spotted at the Shroud of Turin at the Cathedral of Saint John the Baptist.

Another text came through a moment later:

"Found on Gnostic forum: 'Day of Reckoning four days away. Shroud of Turin.' Posted by TP.'"

Ridley focused on the date of the post. The Day of Reckoning, four days away.

The post was dated three days ago.

The Day of Reckoning was *tomorrow*.

## TURIN, ITALY

I t was Brothers Fernando, Zigfried, Gabriel, Luca, Aaron, and Hendrik. And Ridley Shane. The gang was all here at the cathedral.

They'd reviewed the footage on the way over. Tanner Knox was spotted by Saint John's security (their report made at the behest of Pope Leo, who had issued a special request of all Holy institutions to report anyone resembling Knox.)

The footage showed Tanner Knox, limping slightly – no doubt from his recent altercation with Ridley Shane. He milled about the throngs, devout tourists observing the shrine and offering their prayers at the site.

One problem, Tanner's eyes were everywhere *but* the shrine. He was taking pictures of the exits, photographing tourists, snapping shots of the floor and the ceiling. He wasn't using the camera flash, so security couldn't do anything about it. But it was odd behavior and the church staff knew it. It was why they'd made the report.

They entered the basilica of the Cathedral of Saint John the Baptist. A cadre of gendarmerie were stationed before the shroud, which was encased behind a large glass box, fully temperature-controlled. The shroud, purported to be the burial cloth of Jesus Christ, was on display for a limited time for the first time in seven years. Masses of pilgrims swarmed the place.

Each man bore a nearly invisible earpiece with a wire leading to a transmitter worn below the shirt. Every earpiece was outfitted with an ultra-sensitive microphone and location tracker.

The men had split up and scattered throughout the crowd. Ridley waded through the throngs of believers, some lost in holy reverie. He respectfully side-stepped them, keeping his eyes peeled for Tanner Knox.

"Anyone see anything?" said Brother Aaron.

"Negative," said Brother Hendrik.

"Keep your eyes open," said Brother Aaron.

"Thanks for the advice," said Brother Fernando.

Ridley couldn't help but smile. It was exactly like being back with The Jefferson Group.

"First one who spots him gets an ice cream cone," said Brother Luca, the head of the team.

Brother Hendrik's voice chimed in. "You're awfully generous, boss. Sprinkles too?"

"No sprinkles."

"That's too bad. And here I thought there'd be sprinkles. Why am I even here?"

"How you doing, Ridley?" said Brother Luca.

"Alert. Ready."

"Articulate as always," said Brother Aaron. All the Brothers were used to Ridley's terseness by now. It amused them to try and see if they could get more words out of him.

Ridley couldn't help but focus on the shroud before him. There across the cloth was the imprint of a bearded man. Its authenticity was still being debated, but no one could argue that those who came here to see the artifact were forever transformed by it.

A young man stepped through the crowd, determined and focused. He looked straight ahead, not at the shroud, but at the guards who stood like statues in front of it.

Tanner Knox had brown hair. This man was a blonde.

But that face...

"Guys," said Ridley, "heads up."

"What do you see?"

"Not sure. Blonde kid. Heading toward the shroud."

"There are too many people," said Brother Fernando. "Hang on. I'll come and find you."

By virtue of the individual trackers each man wore, each could pinpoint the location of another by a mere glance at a smart watch.

As Ridley kept his eyes trained on the blonde kid, who was suddenly stopped in his tracks by a throng of people crowding close to the shroud, Brother Fernando came up from his left.

"Where is he?"

Ridley motioned with his chin. "Blonde kid."

"Looks like Tanner. He's got the same nose."

Brother Hendrik's voice came through. "I'm coming."

"Let's split up and surround him."

The kid was focused. The look in his eyes was *surreal*. It was... *devout*.

"We're here," came the voice of Brother Gabriel.

Seven men formed a rough circle around the blonde kid.

"Ah yes," said Brother Zigfried, "that's our target alright."

Suddenly, Knox's eyes came alive. They grew wide, and he screamed, "Behold, I cast a fire upon the world!"

With this, he ripped open his shirt to reveal a series of wires and what everyone assumed was explosives.

The crowd dissolved into chaos. The guards drew their weapons.

Tanner held a detonator in his hand.

"The new Jerusalem cometh!" he shouted, edging closer to the shroud.

One of the guards screamed at him to freeze. Tanner stopped.

"Hold," said Brother Luca.

"God, I hope they don't shoot," said Brother Aaron.

"They won't," said Ridley.

"What are you saying, ol' boy?"

"I'm saying his explosives aren't rigged to explode."

"Listen," said Brother Gabriel, "I wouldn't test that theory if I were you."

"Trust me," said Ridley, inching closer to Tanner.

Brother Fernando put a hand on his arm. "Please, think..."

"I'll be fine."

Ridley inched closer.

"Beware the seeds of the Catholic heathens! They have brought forth a tree of poison and pestilence!"

"Easy does it, ol' boy."

"I got this," said Ridley, realizing then that no one, not even the Brothers, had noticed that the wire of the detonator the kid held led down into his front pocket.

Amazing thing, the power of suggestion.

"All hail Cyrus Knox!" shouted Ridley.

Tanner looked at him, his face a frozen mask of confusion. Ridley hauled back and punched the kid square in the jaw. He went down like he'd been paid to do it.

When the guards swarmed in, so did Brother Luca, brandishing orders from His Holiness to release the would-be bomber into his possession. There was, of course, resistance on the part of the guards.

"That was easy," said Brother Hendrik, when they'd finally convinced the guards to let them have Knox.

"Hang on," said Brother Fernando, edging his way toward the

immobile form. He knelt down beside it. He looked as though he were giving Last Rites.

"What are you doing?" said Brother Luca.

Brother Fernando stood up and brushed his hands together. "Just smelling his breath."

Brother Luca stared in confusion.

"Bruce Banner," said Brother Fernando. "He had almond breath. From cyanide."

"And this one?"

Brother Fernando smiled. "Just Colgate."

# VATICAN CITY

They'd convened in the anteroom of the Papal Palace. They sat contemplatively, each one brooding upon what they'd gone through thus far. They held a short prayer session, and Brother Hendrik suggested they bounce ideas back and forth. No one, however, seemed to want to be the first to speak.

Tanner Knox was in a cell in the basement of the palace. He had refused to talk.

Pope Leo entered the room. The men rose from their seats.

"Please, be seated," he commanded.

He stood before the men, his head bowed in what looked like prayer. He picked his head up with a deep breath and began to speak.

"Did you know that in Spain and in Argentina, where I'm from, there is a custom among some of the more...*conservative* types, to offer a plate of charcuterie to guests of the household. Delicious cuts of pork are presented. The gesture is one of warm hospitality. However, the custom has its roots in a rather, shall we say, questionable tradition."

The men looked at each other. It was apparent that no one knew exactly where His Holiness was going with this.

"The custom dates back to the time of the Spanish Inquisition. When a Jew or a Muslim was ostensibly converted, a plate of pork was placed before them. And the newly converted would be invited to take part. That is when the inquisitors would scrutinize the convert for any signs of distaste or disgust, ensuring that the conversion was not a false one."

He paused, allowing the air in the room to thicken with the weight of what he'd just said.

"There are many things," he continued, "about the Catholic Church that leave its opponents great fodder for criticism, and leave the pious flailing for life. We cannot erase our past. But we can fortify our future with righteousness." He looked around the room and smiled warmly. "Why am I telling you this? Because, Brothers, you are not defending a doctrine. You are defending a man. These..." he tugged at his robes, "...these are mere bits of thread. The laws of God: goodness, charity, mercy, and love; these are woven into our hearts. They come from the Master Weaver Himself. And from His Son. That is the man of whom I speak. That is who we are defending. So think not about rituals, sacraments, and bread and wine, but think of the man who wanted to gather the children of Israel as a hen gathers her brood. That is who you must defend. You must defend the man. He would not have allowed deaths such as the ones that have plagued us thus far. Nor would He have condoned them. And He would forgive that man that is locked up in our basement."

"Your Holiness," said Ridley, "I don't have it in my heart to forgive."

"Nor are you expected to, Ridley. But know who you must defend. All of you. Know and recognize who you must defend!"

These last words the pope intoned with such ferocity that each man couldn't help but feel as though the words resonated to the core of their very souls.

The pope turned and left the room.

Ridley stood up, paced the room for a moment.

Then he faced the others. "I understand now," he said, feeling empowered by the pope's words. "The principles of faith," he murmured. Then he looked up and spoke to the others. "It's the principles of the faith. Not the faith itself that we're here to defend. The two are intertwined, but not the same. As we proceed, let us proceed with our *faith* fully defined."

"Friend," said Brother Aaron, "I don't think I've ever seen you like this. What are you suggesting? That we drop our fight?"

"On the contrary," said Ridley.

"The only thing to the contrary," said Brother Hendrik, stopping midway to consider whether he should utter the rest of the sentence, "is holy war."

Ridley Shane didn't disagree.

## ROME, ITALY

Ridley Shane, 35, six-foot-one, head shaved completely bald, sat on the edge of his bed and stared at the wall.

It was an uninteresting piece of masonry. Your standard wall, hastily erected, functional. Painted a drab green like the color of a bad piece of meat. It wasn't the wall, really, that he stared at, but a certain crack that ran along a small portion of it. It was about four inches in length, probably just small enough to pass inspection.

Who had designed this prison anyway? Was it some architectural major's thesis on the power of motel construction to induce feelings of extreme desperation in its inhabitants? The worst part of it all was that he felt as though he could eventually get used to the blandness, the sparseness of decor, the feeling that the room had spent a great deal of its life submerged in some murky lagoon. The walls spoke of countless ages of anonymity. He could definitely get used to it, and what's worse, he didn't mind that fact.

But back to that crack that ran along toward the ceiling. It was near the corner by the oval table that served no purpose other than a perfunctory prop for a lamp that illuminated no more than a six-inch perimeter around its shade.

The crack was in the shape of a finger that curled slightly. He hadn't thought of that finger in ages, it seemed. And now, here it was, pointing up and curved like a small hook. They'd joked about it then. The witch finger, she called it, back when his life was headed in some other, still-unknown part of the universe...

---

## BARDSTOWN, KENTUCKY

Ridley Shane, 23, six-foot-one, head full of thick, dark brown locks like one of the Beatles, sat on a rock in the park with a Bible on his lap.

"You'll go blind reading that stuff," said a female voice.

Normally, Ridley wouldn't have been distracted from his reading for anything. For some reason, he had an inability to concentrate on anything that didn't keep his mind active. When he read, it was full-throttle. He dove into books, and he swam deep within their pages. He let the words clog his ears and stop his breath. And this book in particular. This one that he'd read and re-read so many pages of and contemplated endlessly. He couldn't comprehend where he'd found the time to read anything else, so steeped was he in Bible study. It was like those stories of folks snatched up by aliens and deposited back on earth minutes later, only to find that they'd spent hours onboard the mothership.

But this one passage puzzled him. Jesus and the spikenard. He couldn't make sense of it, or how it fit in to the wisdom and mystery that surrounded it. He could not swim through it, could not comprehend its meaning. Hence the distraction.

"Excuse me?" he said to the girl, noticing at first the luscious auburn hair that fell around her shoulders in bunches and reflected sunlight from the tips. Wasn't there a line from a Beach Boys song about that?

"That's the Bible, ain't it?" Brooklyn accent. Like a cartoon.

"It is."

"Right. And so I said that stuff will make you go blind. You should be reading some good stuff. James Joyce. Moby Dick. Danielle Steele. Literary ice cream. Not that stuff. It's so redundant."

There was a playful way about her—maybe it was the Danielle Steele line—that gave him the calmness in his spirit not to take offense at what she was saying. He was as brash about the Bible as she was about, well, things that weren't the Bible.

"Redundant?" he said, playfully challenging her.

"Sure. What morality can you find in there that you can't find in any great literature?"

"You know," he said, squinting at her when she moved a foot to the left and the sunlight streamed into his eyes, "you speak like some kind of mutant."

Her eyes widened. "A mutant?"

"Yeah, a mixture of highbrow and lowlife."

"Well, I don't have to stand here and take this, I can go turn on some opera if I want to listen to a strange guy yelling at me. What are you doing here anyway? Forming an intimate relationship with that rock?"

Her smile seemed to stretch to eternity. It made him want to look away.

"I'm studying."

"Studying what?"

"To become a priest, if you really want to know."

She folded her arms. "Really?"

He nodded.

"Now that's very interesting."

"Some say."

"What led you to that?"

He shrugged. "Promise to my mom? I don't know. I just... wanted to."

"Huh."

"If you don't mind," he said, flipping open the Good Book once again.

"Let me ask you something," she said, putting a hand on her hip. "I've been watching you for about five minutes. I was over yonder, contemplating life, the universe, and everything, and I looked up and saw this handsome young fellow reading a book. And so I thought, let me get closer to this young fellow. Because, you see, I like guys who read." Here she tilted her head, and again he needed to look away.

And then she did this thing with her finger. She brought it up to her lips, as if she were pulling out a stock mannerism from a hackneyed bag of mime tricks—the eyes turned up, the finger to the lips as if in deep thought—and he noticed that her finger was curved in a hook.

"Hmm," she said, hook finger to lips, "I wonder if this nice-looking young chap would like to come with me someplace where there are fewer bugs and have some lunch or coffee? And maybe we could... ooh, I don't know... talk about books maybe?" She shrugged.

He smiled.

"Then I came over and saw you reading that, that thing there, that Bible thingy, and I thought, 'gee, why would the Good Lord above choose such a devastatingly handsome young gent to be His prophet on earth?' Then it struck me. Yes, of course! A handsome prophet! That's just the ticket! Nobody would listen to you if you were some ugly little spud with a bulbous nose and an aggravated case of acne."

"Your point being? You want to have lunch?"

She put both hands to her hips now. "Whatever gave you that idea?"

It was her smile that led to his assent. And if nothing else, he wanted the story behind that finger.

---

"IT'S REALLY NOT THAT INTERESTING," she said.

Ridley turned his diner coffee cup so that he could drink from the non-lipsticked side. "I didn't mean to pry."

"Oh, no," she said, "I know that. I'm just saying it's not that interesting. We had a sump behind the church where I grew up. You had to climb this small hill behind the church parking lot and then it dipped and there was the sump. My girlfriend Jenn and I smoked cigarettes there. Well, she smoked, I watched. And there were these guys who'd steal dirty magazines and read them there. I saw one once. Disgusted me forever. Anyway, every winter there'd inevitably be a week or so where the sump would freeze over. Like, solid. And you could actually skate on it. Well, one time, in the middle of a double camel or whatever the hell you call it, I slipped and jammed my finger into the ice. The doctor, bless his quack heart, set it wrong. And it was just a little messed up. Years later, I broke it again when I jammed it into my boyfriend's '72 Skylark after an argument. The doctor said it was too messed up to set properly. He said, 'I can set it in any way you want, but you'll never be able to move it again.' So, being young and idiotic, I said, 'Just give me a witch finger.' He said, 'A witch finger?' I said, 'Yeah, make it curved like a hook so I can still pick up pretzels with it.' And after an hour of trying to talk me out of it, he somehow became convinced that I was logical in my decision-making process and he set it like this. And there you have it. Told you it wasn't interesting."

He laughed. "That was one of the most interesting stories about a finger I've ever heard in my life."

"You think? Maybe I'll have it published."

"You should."

"Ok," she said, taking her cup in her folded hands and leaning her elbows on the table, "*quid pro quo*, doctor. Have you seen *Silence of the Lambs*? Creepy as hell, right? Anyway, now you have to tell me something. Why a priest?"

"Because I'm terrible at math."

One raised eyebrow.

"It was the first thing I could think of. I told you, I really don't know why I want to be a priest. I kinda feel like it's something I always wanted but could never put my finger on. Then one day, I stood in the sacristy of St. Elizabeth's Church. I was an altar boy and I was assisting in the First Communion ceremony. It was a small church in a small community, and so there was something like twenty kids there. I had forgotten something. I swear I can't remember what it was. I think we were one chalice short or something. Then I heard twenty kids in unison saying the Lord's Prayer. All twenty in these loud, earnest voices that spoke as one." He paused, staring at the table, as the menu blurred. He dabbed his eyes once with his napkin. "The walls kind of fell away at that moment. It was so pure, so loving, so innocent, all those voices praying at once."

"How old were you?" she asked softly.

"Fourteen. I didn't know what happened. I mean, I hadn't even really finished puberty yet. Here was this profound experience. It was too much. But I knew at that moment that I couldn't walk away from the Church for anything." He paused again, his mind peacefully blank, then added with a smile, "I was in its orbit."

RIDLEY SHANE, 30, six-foot-one, head freshly shaved, stood in the main courtyard of the Abbey of Our Lady of Gethsemani. The Kentucky sun streamed down, staining the white slate walls the color of yellow joy. God was in His palace, seated on His golden throne, and all was right.

He had been a postulant, a candidate for membership of the Order of Cistercians of the Strict Observance—he preferred the name "Trappist", which had a less elitist ring to it—for six months, and was on his way to see the novice director about his admittance to the next phase of monastic life – the Novitiate. From that point on, he'd be officially accepted into the order of the monkhood. For the next two years, he'd live under strict guidance by the novice director, and live like a monk, as a monk, with the monks.

He paced the grounds, nervously fidgeting with the belt on his robes, muttering quick devotions to quell the sense of anxiety he had in his gut.

Then he saw the crack in the wall. It looked like...

He turned his head away from it, thinking that, in his mind, he was turning away from the memory of *her*.

His breath quickened in his chest. They'd been together, once. He'd slept with her just once. But he'd looked into her eyes and saw everything that he was lacking in his life. It was the connection he needed.

But he was twenty-three then, as was she. And they had been in the process of discovering themselves. And she had this laugh that lit him up. And she put her hand on his chest once, and felt his heart, and she told him that she wanted to live there, inside him. And he told her that the space had always been there, carved out for her a long time ago.

But they were young. And it fell to pieces because their love was too big, too profound for either of them. And they broke up, tearfully but mutually.

And now, here was that crack in the wall.

He fell to his knees.

"Lord," he whispered, "why did you show that to me? Is this a test?"

The fear entered him unbidden.

So much sin in the world. No use hiding from it. It creeped in through the cracks.

Through the crack...

What good was he here? If he was out there, maybe he couldn't save them all. But he could save her.

And he went to his closet in his cell and dug out his layperson clothes and put them on. They were loose—he hadn't realized he'd lost so much weight. And he left the place without telling anyone. He ran from it. He ran to her.

---

MISTER CLEAN, she called him. Turns out, she liked bald men. Who knew? He kept it for her. He was actually grateful when he saw he was prematurely balding on the back of his head. It gave him an excuse for that twice-a-week ritual with the electric buzzer. And she liked it and she stroked it and cooed over him and gave him every reason he had to be alive.

And one big reason. They named him Jake, short for Jacob.

Jake, who'd developed a head of thin, blonde curls and a sweet way of blinking when he smiled (he had her eyes). She took him out to pick up a couple of steaks and a bottle of Merlot for a nice, relaxing Friday night with *Ghostbusters* on the VCR and Jake in his crib early. But there was a drunk who didn't stop at the intersection.

RIDLEY SHANE, 31, six-foot-one, bald, stood at the grave of his wife and child.

HE'D KEPT his scalp clean. He often told people it was in her honor, but in truth, he'd grown accustomed to it. It was part of who he was now, and that bit of irony thrilled him. No longer was he the passive, contemplative monk in training. Now he was just a six-foot warrior with a mile-long stare and a chip on his shoulder the size of Wisconsin.

It was the third anniversary of the deaths of Anna and Jacob. He found himself drinking his way toward the gutter in Grover's Pub on Shelter Avenue. Every sip of acid burned away another memory but left the feelings.

He stumbled out of the pub around ten. Somewhere during his amblings, he'd managed to insult someone, somewhere, and earned himself a sock to the jaw. He spent an hour—maybe two— lying in the doorway of a closed drugstore, sobbing hot tears, his lip swelling, the blood running down the front of his collar.

An angel appeared before him. It stooped down and offered its hand.

"Take it," said the angel.

Through tears, Ridley Shane stuttered the words, "Forgive me."

"Come with me," said Father Emilio Garcia.

THE FUTURE POPE was visiting his family in New Jersey. He couldn't sleep that night and had gone out for a stroll, certain of his safety in the Catholic neighborhood, dressed as he was. The pitiful sight of the man in the drug store doorway had wrenched his heart, and he picked up the man and brought him home. His family objected, as probably any family would, but Father Garcia's influence was a gift from God, and he used it for God. And he took the man in despite his family's protests, offering a word or two from Scripture as something to contemplate.

*Whatsoever you do to the least of my brothers, that you do unto me.*

---

RIDLEY SHANE CONSIDERED his memory of the previous night a minor miracle in itself.

"You're *wandering*?" the priest said.

"If that's a synonym for homeless, no. I was running from ghosts."

The priest nodded. He had an aura, the way a mild-smelling cologne might come off a man's body. It was spiritual contentedness that came off him. "Tell me more about your ghosts."

"There's not much to tell."

But he did tell. And he realized just how much there was to tell. The way she licked a wooden spoon after mixing brownie batter and then dipped it back into the bowl. The way she blew her nose with both elbows pointed outward. The sounds she made when she was playful, or moody, or jealous, or regretful—those sounds you can only know through marriage. And there was so much to tell about Jacob, things he missed about that short and precious time he knew the child. The gurgles, the inquisitiveness of his eyes, the sounds of joy and hunger and fear and love.

Ridley Shane wept, his head on Father Garcia's shoulder.

When it was over, he sat silent, elbows on his knees, hands clasped, and he confessed to the priest.

"I feel nothing," he said. "Nothing for God. Nothing for any of it. I have no faith left."

The future pope closed his eyes and breathed deeply.

"Is that all you can do?" Ridley spat.

The priest opened his eyes. "Excuse me?"

"That's all you have? You rape me of my emotions and then you sit there mute while I'm drifting away?"

Father Garcia's mouth hung open. He shook his head.

"Never mind," said Ridley Shane, rising. "You sit there silent. You and God are a perfect match. See you around, Father."

# ROME, ITALY

Ridley Shane, 35, six-foot-one, bald, sat on a bed in a crappy motel just outside Vatican City, staring at a crack in the wall.

He was ashamed of himself. The holy man just on the other side of the Vatican wall had earned his position. He was the same man as he'd always been, a kind, loving, sternly spiritual presence on earth. And he, Ridley, was a sinner and a fugitive from the Church.

He remembered his wanderings, beginning with a flirtation with atheism. Until he realized that he couldn't square that nothingness with the somethingness of the world in which he lived. And so he flirted with one religion and then another. And he came back to Christianity and found that all the man-made institutions couldn't wrap their doctrines around the mystery of Jesus Christ. Until that day when he said, without a trace of irony, to hell with it all. If he couldn't follow any one religion, so be it. He would believe in God and Jesus and the Holy Spirit. And it would stay there. And it was enough to know that his life could be fulfilled by merely believing.

He'd gotten work campaigning for the future President

Zimmer, who would in time let him in on the secret of The Jefferson Group. And he met Cal and Daniel and the rest of their team, all friends soon after. Trusting Ridley's sense of justice, his convictions, and his air as one who had walked through fire and emerged intact, he made the young campaigner an offer to join a branch of the CIA. And Ridley Shane was reborn as an agent, impressing his superiors enough to be assigned some of the most secret operations of the Zimmer administration. As an agent, Ridley Shane had the country's highest clearance, an honor shared by every member of the elite Jefferson Group, of whose existence only he and a privileged few were aware.

And when the name Father Emilio Garcia came up in the news, when the former archbishop of Argentina was elected pope, the old fear returned.

Not fear—guilt.

And a sense that an act of contrition was necessary. He spoke to the president, who arranged for a trip to Vatican City.

It was there, here, a mere three years ago, that he fell at the holy man's feet. A witness described the scene: Two guards rushing to remove him; the pope's arms outstretched.

And the words from Ridley Shane's throat, introducing him now as they introduced him all those years ago:

"Forgive me."

---

THE CRACK in the wall was invisible now, as the sun was setting. The shadows in the room grew black and spread over the space like a fog. And Ridley Shane licked his lips.

*Holy war*, he thought.

It was as good an excuse for war as any. He hadn't come this far in life to sit on the side and report the news. He needed to participate.

He needed to defend.

He dialed Brother Gabriel.

"Hello, Ridley."

"I need to talk to the Brothers."

"His Holiness spoke fire today."

"Indeed," said Ridley. "And I for one felt the power of his words." It sounded like someone else's voice, someone steadfast and unbreakable.

"We were all a little shaken by his tone."

"I know. So was I. But then I remembered why I came here. I finally realized it. I've chosen the role of defender of the faith. And now I am going to act the part to its fullest."

"I see it is now you who is speaking fire."

The tone was not without a playful bit of mockery. Ridley brushed it off as a confused and cautious response to his own tone. Even he didn't know how to react to this sharpened mind-set. He'd reached a nexus of understanding here in this tiny cave of a motel room. And why not? He'd had a religious experience in the sacristy of an obscure little church back home. Why not a motel room?

"Brother Gabriel, I need to tell you something."

"I am listening."

"Are you alone?"

"At the moment, yes."

"I am telling you this because I have faith in your confidence." He paused, unsure his throat could carry the weight of the words he was about to deliver. He licked his lips and delivered them straight and unbroken: "I believe we may have an informer in our midst."

## TILLINGS NECK, NY

Detective Maddox was grateful for plain clothes and an unmarked car as he exited the Dunkin' Donuts on Route 4. He remembered the looks he used to get, and the remarks just above a stage whisper, followed by chuckles. He just wasn't in the mood for cop and donut jokes at the moment.

Not that there was anyone around to make them, unless you counted the poor guy behind the counter working the graveyard shift. A Friday night at two in the a.m.; the entire town was deader than Latin.

He got into his car and sighed. A mere twenty minutes ago he was blissfully asleep, right before Sarah nudged him awake with a craving for a Boston Creme. He'd gotten up without a word, like it was his job.

He started the car and then squinted up the road. Williams Street was just up ahead. That's where the library was, and just up the road from that was the spot where the kid – Scott Hampton – had encountered the dying Jofar Aslan.

He nibbled at his thumbnail for a moment.

"Aw hell," he muttered, and started up the road toward the library.

*Let's pretend that I'm Aslan,* he thought. *What the hell am I doing here?*

And the answer came: *I'm not getting books. The books I have here in my car are from my own collection, purchased through Amazon with a stolen credit card, delivered to the doorstep of the cardholder. I intercepted them.*

*From there, my steps are obscured for a while. But shortly after receiving these books in my possession, I drove past here, with the library on my left. Then I took a right up onto Canal Street. There I saw the church. I got out... here.*

Maddox slowed the car as he approached the church, St. Matthew's Roman Catholic.

Small town churches are typically quaint buildings, clapboard meeting house-type structures belonging more to the days of puritanism than these times. Maddox imagined the type of place where folks attended day-long services, where a preacher in a wide-brimmed hat bellowed about hellfire and damnation and devils in our midst. This was no such place. It was a small building, but a shrunken miniature of a much larger structure of spires and stained glass and gothic architecture – like someone had left St. Patrick's cathedral in the dryer too long, painted it white, and stuck it here where no one would find it.

Any moment now he would get a text from Sarah, but it was gnawing at him, the sight of this building. He pulled up to the spot where Aslan had stopped to take pictures. He'd been here investigating Aslan's death so many times, both in person and on Google maps, that it was like a remote office. But that was in the daytime. At two in the morning, this place was surreal. Not even the wind was awake.

It was amazing how the surreality of the situation gave him a new perspective. Why hadn't he come here at this time of night more often? Why hadn't he taken more advantage of that kind of alien viewpoint one can only get when one sees something in a literally different light?

He left the car running and approached the building on foot. An ugly feeling of vulnerability crept over him. His 9mm was in the glove box.

*I'm Jofar Aslan. I'm a twenty-seven-year-old miscreant from New Jersey. I have a brother named Mehmet who moved to Turkey and that's the last time anyone heard from him.*

*I'm standing here with my camera, taking pictures of this church. Why?*

A little bug in his brain fluttered its wings. It did so whenever there was a question that was unanswered, and the answer carried weight that could break a case.

*Then a red SUV drives past and shoots me.*

No, dammit! Back up. You're standing here taking pictures. Freeze that SUV. They're not needed in the film yet.

*I'm standing here with my camera...*

He positioned himself in the exact spot on Canal Street, just across from the church.

He had a view of the place just slightly off-center. The circular stained glass window hung over the arched entrance. He squinted at it.

*What's here that interests me? Am I casing the joint?*

He clenched his teeth and breathed heavily through his nose. The bug in his brain fluttered its wings.

*What's here that I'm so interested in? The stained-glass window...*

The answer came to him, unbidden. He had to stop for a moment and think where the chain of thought had originated.

It originated with a flash memory of the first time he'd arrived on the scene and saw the drops of Jofar Aslan's blood on the ground. One of them was in the shape of a heart. Sarah always kept a lookout for naturally-occurring heart shapes, seeing them as signs or whatever. It was her habit to point them out to him. A heart-shaped cloud, a heart-shaped knot in a tree, a heart-shaped cookie crumb. She'd grab his elbow and point them out to him as if he really saw the same significance as she did. He'd always feigned interest. After all, he wasn't stupid. It was his duty as a husband to feign interest.

But something had happened to him by the sheer repeated exposure to this sort of pattern-seeking: He'd begun to notice the damned things everywhere. Heart-shaped dings in park benches, heart-shaped acorns on the ground. He'd taken to snapping shots of them with his cell phone and sending them to her.

And now he remembered when he saw the heart-shaped blood stain, and how he had to stop himself from snapping a shot of it and sending it to her. Too grotesque. He'd appreciate this one on his own.

He'd noticed something else: That if he took the picture of it from the angle he was standing in at the time, the time of day being late, his shadow would have stretched long past the stain on the ground. He thought at the time that it would have been an interesting shot to have gotten, this heart-shaped blood stain with his long shadow astride it, stretching off toward the church.

He looked up. The sun hitting the church around that time would have hit that stain glass window pretty much head-on. He imagined what it might look like inside the church when it did. Probably something fairly spectacular.

He remembered something in one of the books they found in Aslan's car. He couldn't remember the title. But there was something in it he'd found while randomly thumbing through them. It was an illustration: a circle with seven points on its circumference, and a symmetrical pattern of shapes like diamonds situated at these points. He looked up at the circular stained-glass window. Seven points on it, each with a diamond-like pattern extending toward it.

Maybe Aslan...

*I'm on my way inside the church to photograph the effect of the sun shining through the stained-glass, but I never make it inside. I stop to photograph the outside first, for continuity's sake. Or for the sake of sheer aesthetic. It is, after all, a beautiful place. Then a red SUV drives up...*

Maddox was kicking himself now. Why hadn't he followed this train of logic sooner when he was standing there that day with his own shadow pointing him in the direction of a possible answer?

He needed to get inside that church at that same time of day, with the sun shining brightly, and that time of day was a long way off. Another thought came on the heels of that one, and he pulled out his phone to check that day's weather forecast...

Cloudy.

"Shit," he muttered.

His phone beeped.

From Sarah: *"You OK, my love? Where's my donut?"*

Giving one last look at the church, he turned and headed back to his car.

## ROME, ITALY

He'd been a lone wolf all his life, Ridley Shane.

Walking along the streets of Rome, he saw passersby as if through a mask. There was a time in his life where this sort of anonymity frightened him. Now, after years with the CIA, he preferred to be an obscurity, someone who blended into scenery.

He watched Beatricia Nespoli leave the Church of Saint Gregory VII, then followed every step she took.

It hadn't been easy tracking her down. He had to get a word to the president, through Daniel Briggs, and had to do it in such a way that seemed innocuous. Just a little background info gathering. Not at all suspicious. *Not like I'm trying to put a tail on a possible rat in the organization or anything.*

He knew, instinctively, how it would play out. Word would get to Nespoli that the president wanted to know her current whereabouts. Nespoli would, in turn, be sure not to make any bizarre turns until she was sure the eyes were off her. This left Ridley a perfect opportunity to trail her throughout a normal daily routine, without any fear of winding up in some situation he didn't want to be in – one, say, involving electric cattle prods.

The church was a rather modern structure of intersecting

panels and sharp-angled gables. It was as if a Puritan-era house of clapboard siding was suddenly inflated to the size of a cathedral, given a sprucing up, and finished off by a sprinkle of divine tears.

She walked down Via del Cottolengo, past an apartment complex, then made the sharp left where the street ended. There was no right turn to make. The street was claustrophobically narrow, made more so by the two opposing blocks of apartments on either side.

He stalked her around the corner, taking a moment to linger at the turn, one shoulder against the corner building. A sharp smell of eucalyptus wafted under his nose. From where, he couldn't tell. It was a breath from some grove somewhere. The air up to that point had been stale and still.

He rounded the corner and spotted her up ahead, halted before a locked electrical cabinet that obviously housed the power controls for one of the apartments. Though her back was to him, he could tell she was fumbling through her purse.

He was suddenly aware of exposure and moved behind a parked delivery van. Poking his head out slightly, he had a clear view of her just beneath the van's side view mirror.

She turned and walked up to the cabinet, a key in hand. She opened it as one would a bus locker, and extracted a brown paper parcel. This she did without any glances up or down the street, as if the action was the most normal thing she could be doing at that time.

This didn't tie in with his theory about how she would move if she knew she was being watched. Here was a perfectly out-of-the-ordinary act, executed in the plain of day, in a bland section of town.

She put the parcel in her purse and continued walking up the street, making a left in order to head back to the main road from whence she'd come.

He picked up his pace when she rounded the corner, not stopping once he made it there.

That was a mistake. One unworthy of the greenest rookie agent. He later attributed it to mental fatigue. Plus, it had been a while since he tailed a suspect. Both of these things constituted a good enough rationalization for the gaffe. He would from then on be sure to exercise the highest precautions, he was sure of that.

Right now, however, he merely froze in place. For Beatricia Nespoli was waiting for him.

She had a pistol in her hand.

## ROME, ITALY

"Give me one good reason why I shouldn't shoot you," she said, lowering the pistol to a place just left of the center of his chest.

"For one thing," he said calmly, "I'm willing to bet *you* don't have a reason to shoot. Second, we're kind of surrounded by apartments. You don't think someone can see us?"

"People in this area of the world mind their own business, Mr. Shane. They were raised to do so. It is a matter of survival. You Americans are privileged that way, not to know conditions under which one must *choose* to survive."

"I suppose you're going to tell me that war does that to a people."

"War, religious conflict, day to day struggles."

"I've seen all those things. Tell me more about privilege."

She cocked the pistol. "Why are you following me?"

"Don't you know?" he said. His frustration over not knowing what was happening made him feel surly. At this point, he wasn't even sure whether he gave a damn if she fired the thing or not.

"Why are you following me, Mr. Shane?"

"You're acting awfully suspicious for a woman who knows

she's being watched. What did you take from that electrical cabinet?"

"None of your business."

Ridley felt a laugh coming on. And then it came. Full-chested. He doubled over. He imagined how it would end for him. The end of Ridley Shane. The end of a life of searching, seeking, praying, fighting, hacking his way through the dark, living, loving, and losing, and *this* was how it would end: a woman plugging him in the chest with a handgun in an alley between two apartment buildings. In Italy. It was so... *unpoetic*. The absurdity of the situation struck him like an anvil to the back of the head.

"What are you laughing at?" she said, bending slightly to look at his face.

He seized the moment. With two hands, one to the inner part of the wrist, the other to the back of her clutching hand, he boxed her hard. She let out a sharp cry. The gun went flying. For good measure, he grabbed her other wrist. He knew the gun hand was at least momentarily incapacitated.

"I'll break it," he said, holding her wrist up above her head. It killed him to do this to a woman. Of course he wouldn't actually follow through on the threat. He'd been raised better than that. But she didn't know that.

"You already broke my other hand," she whimpered.

"It's fine. Put a little ice on it and take some Advil."

"Let go!" she cried.

He did so. Her hand went down immediately and cradled her wounded wrist.

"What did you take from the cabinet?"

She tightened her lips and gritted her teeth behind them. She slowly went to her purse. Ridley stiffened at this, letting his body language speak for itself: *No sudden moves,* it said.

She extracted a brown paper parcel about the size and shape

of a brick. She was about to open it, when she suddenly looked around, fearful.

"Not here," she said.

"I thought you said people here mind their own business."

She shook her head vigorously. "No, this is different. Not here."

"Where then?" he said with a tone of obvious impatience.

"The church," she said flatly. "Walk with me there."

---

IF THE EXTERIOR of the Parrocchia di San Gregorio VII was deceiving as a place of Roman Catholic worship, the interior certainly made up for it. Ornate, cavernous, with stone pillars and an altar of marble, the church still retained elements of modern architecture. But the spirit of the place was ancient. It was a place that demanded, as most churches of this size and structure do, awed silence. Even the air felt like it was of another time.

Confessionals lined the left side of the church at ten-foot intervals. Silently, she walked toward one. Ridley followed. She entered one side and he the other. It occurred to him then how odd it was that she chose the priest's side, while allowing him to take the seat for the confessor. After all, it was she who was revealing to him, not the other way around.

She slid open the partition. Soft light from an automatic bulb bathed the lower half of her face. She was lovely in the glow, which was red like a pre-storm sunrise.

He heard the rustle of paper, and then a tearing sound.

She slid something through the confession aperture.

It was an old, dusty brick.

"Take it," she said softly.

He did so. It was lighter than he'd expected.

"Open it."

He looked at her and she nodded. He turned the brick over in his hands and noticed, in the fire light, a groove that ran along the side. He fidgeted with it for a second, and suddenly it gave. He slid off the top like a pencil box. Something that rested in the hollow of it glimmered. He put the two brick halves on his lap and lifted the thing out.

It was a circular piece of gold, shimmering hot sparks in the glow of the confessional. The size of a half-dollar, it had been etched along its circumference, on both sides, with something unfamiliar to him: strange symbols that were like glyphs or ancient runes. He looked up at her, not knowing what to say.

Her lips parted, and he heard the dry smack as they did. "Men are going to die for that."

He looked at the thing again. Then back at her. "I don't understand."

"You seek the Nicene Cipher," she said, her voice wavering.

"Yes," he answered, transfixed by the purity of the moment.

"That is its key. Without it, the document is gibberish."

He was dumbfounded. He felt his palms becoming sweaty. His fingers trembled as he replaced the disc back into the hollow of the brick.

"That brick," said Beatricia, "was hidden in plain sight, as you say. The disc changed hands from protector to protector, down through the ages, until the year 1583, when it was encased in that brick and laid within the foundation of the Basilica, in the North side of the wall in Saint Peter's tomb. It has been unknowingly guarded ever since."

"What am I supposed to do with this?"

"I leave that up to you, Mr. Shane."

"Why is it up to me?"

"Because you have seen fit to involve yourself in this matter. I was here to guide you to where I needed you to be. But since you could not leave me be until my plan was completed, I leave this explosive device in your hands. But I'm warning you, Mr. Shane, the rest of my plan is unchanged."

"And what is the rest of your plan, if I may ask?"

She took a breath and tucked a strand of hair behind her ear. "*San Gregorio*," she said, making the sign of the cross. "Do you know of the man for whom this church is named?"

Ridley shook his head slowly.

A slight smile appeared on her face, as if she relished the opportunity to impart a bit of knowledge. "Saint Gregory, as you would call him, was a pope who reigned during the eleventh century. He is revered for restoring purity to the Church. He abolished practices such as the selling and buying of sacred offices – simony – and of civil influences on the Catholic Church. He cleansed the Church, much like Christ casting moneylenders from the temple."

"Why are you telling me this?"

"Because that is my plan, Mr. Shane. I came here earlier today to ask Saint Gregory for his intervention. With the discovery of the Nicene Cipher, the Church will crumble. I must keep that from happening."

Her voice quivered with rage. Her eyes pierced the semi-darkness.

"I am going to kill the man who killed my love, my Mehmet. I won't rest until I do. And I won't allow anyone to interfere. Good day, Mr. Shane, and may God keep you."

With this, she exited the confessional, leaving him sitting there, a thousand thoughts vying for prominence inside his brain.

He looked down at the opened brick and its coin of gleaming gold. Her little metaphor was apt: he felt as though there was a bomb sitting in his lap.

## TILLINGS NECK, NY

C hief Detective Len Maddox didn't have faith in anything, except for small miracles. These included getting an extra Snickers bar out of the vending machine (happened once); or an open line at the cash register at Shaw's (happened three times). He also knew about the tiny miracle that jittered in place, encased within a larger vessel that once accepted his hand in marriage. He was grateful for all these things, these small miracles. He had faith in them.

And so when the clouds cleared and the sun shone, precisely around the time that Jofar Aslan had been snapping photos of the exterior of Saint Matthew's, his faith in small things was once again renewed. He wasn't sure if there was anything or anyone up there pulling the strings, but he could have some faith that there was. It was as simple as that. The mind of Len Maddox was already too complex a structure without adding epistemology to the mix.

He walked into the church. Altar boys milled about, taking candles and flowers away. There had been a funeral. The boys chatted quietly, chuckling irreverently, with a hush from one of them every so often. Maddox's footsteps reverberated off the high ceilings. He looked behind him and saw the stained-glass window. A *mandala* is what his wife would have called it. She had a coloring book full of the same types of symmetrical, circular patterns. He looked around the church and saw the multicolored pattern thrown about. It was an odd effect. It should have been concentrated like a single shadow upon the floor, but instead, the light dispersed around the room. Perhaps the panels of stained-glass were slightly convex, which would allow for the light passing through to refract. All around the church were the seven points of glaring red. He sidestepped his way between the pews slowly. He didn't want to be caught in the awkward act of crossing the altar without genuflecting.

There was a glowing patch of red near a baptismal font. He walked over to it. Next to the font, on the floor, was a pattern in one of the smooth stones there. It was a red crosshatch. Nothing significant, just a pattern laid in to the stone. Several other stones like it had been laid nearby, but only one had the crosshatch.

Then he realized something. He looked at his watch. Then back at the floor.

In a few minutes, the red glow from the window would be over that very stone with the crosshatch pattern. He took a seat in the pew and checked his phone while he waited.

It was one of Maddox's small miracles. The sun moved, the glow shifted and moved with it. Over the crosshatched stone it went. And when it did, the red glow blotted out the crosshatch pattern, rendering it invisible.

All that was there was a word in faint gray letters. Small enough not to be noticed if you weren't here at the right time, on the right kind of day, in the right place, looking at the right stone.

It said, *DUX*.

He quickly moved to another part of the church where points of red light was focused. This time he found the word, *FUGIENS*.

He scrambled to all seven points of red light that floated with the unceasing motion of the sun. At each point was a stone with the crosshatched pattern, one that was obscured and revealed another word. He fumbled for his memo pad and jotted down the words as he found them:

DUX FUGIENS HABERIS ZELOTYPOS KARUS SIC QUAM

He took a seat in a pew and studied the words. It didn't take him long to figure out that this was Latin, and that the words could be arranged in a certain way to make some sort of syntactical sense.

In a couple of minutes, he gave up trying to figure it out with Google alone. He'd need more help.

By this time, the sun had moved on, and the refracted lights traveled along the floor to begin their journey up the walls.

# VATICAN CITY

He sat in the pope's private garden, awaiting the arrival of the Brothers. He didn't for one moment let the brick out of his sight. He hadn't the whole way here. He'd carried it out of the church like it was pure fire in his hands. He couldn't help but be aware of its presence at all times.

He was able to be somewhat amused now as he recalled the priest entering the confessional and finding him there. And how he fumbled an excuse in broken Italian, and gathered up the brick with the key to the cipher and stumbled out with enough apologies to mark him the guiltiest man in all of Rome.

He became aware of a presence. He looked up to see His Holiness smiling down on him.

He stood up, the brick lay at his feet.

Without a word, Pope Leo bent down and picked up the brick. He looked at it from all angles, as one wishing to purchase an antique might scrutinize the item for defects. He breathed heavily through his nose as he did. Then he separated the two halves. His eyes lit up when what was inside was revealed. His eyes then turned to Ridley.

"Was there violence in attaining this?"

The eyes were piercing, powerful.

"Yes, Your Eminence."

The pope took a deep breath and let it out with a mumbled prayer. Ridley could barely hear it, but it was clear enough. And he remembered enough from his days studying for the priesthood to recognize it:

*Father, forgive them, for they know not what they do.*

He then spoke to Ridley. "I am going to keep this in a safe place."

"Your Eminence, I beg your pardon," said Ridley. "There is a price on your head already. What good is it to keep the object of their greed near you?"

"Peace, Ridley" answered Pope Leo. "Peace. You must trust me. Here in this fortress," he held up his hands and looked around to signify the immensity of the Papal Palace, "a treasure is much safer than in the hands of any one person."

The pope turned and walked back toward the palace.

"Did I miss something?" said Brother Zigfried.

Ridley, startled, turned sharply toward the voice. The monk stood in full habit, hands clasped before him.

"There is a woman," said Ridley, "by the name of Beatricia Nespoli. She is supposedly here to help guide us."

"Guide us?"

"President Zimmer sent her."

"I see. And you said 'supposedly'?"

"Yes. She's a veritable encyclopedia, and I assume she has some contacts, though I don't quite know how she fits in to the big picture. All I know is that she can't be trusted entirely."

"Really, now?" asked Brother Zigfried.

"I thought we might have a spy within our midst. I'm not sure it isn't her. Plus, she has her own agenda. Too much to go into at the moment. But let's just say that her goals and our goals intersect at a key point: Mehmet Aslan."

"How so?"

"She wants to avenge his death," replied Ridley.

The monk bowed his head slightly in thought. "Do you know this man Knox? The guy with the fake bomb?"

"What about him?" asked Ridley.

"I think we should track down the father, don't you?"

"I think that would be a good idea."

"And," said Brother Zigfried, "if this leads in the direction you say it leads, then—"

"Then," said Ridley, "it means Beatricia Nespoli knows what we need to know."

"Precisely," said Brother Zigfried. "Any chance of inviting her for a little chat? Nothing violent. Just... persuasive."

Ridley thought for a moment. "I think I can get her to meet me—or us—somewhere."

"The other chaps are on their way here. Is the old man going to brief us?"

"He just left," said Ridley, rubbing the top of his bald head.

"You put anything on that? Aftershave or lotion of any kind?"

Ridley smiled. "Rubbing alcohol."

"You're kidding."

"No."

"Huh. Well then, if the old man isn't going to brief us, then I suppose I shall return to contemplation."

"No," said Ridley. "We need to act. And we need to act now. Listen, let's say that Nespoli kills the guy who killed Mehmet Aslan. I'm pretty sure that takes care of our business. But there's something greater at stake: The Nicene Cipher. We need to find it. I've... obtained the key to decoding it."

"You what?" Brother Zigfried exclaimed. "Where on earth—?"

"Never mind that right now. The details don't matter. His Holiness just took it away from me to put it somewhere. For safe keeping, he says."

"Oh dear."

"And they're after it," Ridley pronounced.

"Who is?"

"I don't know. Whoever killed Mehmet Aslan. Whoever is hell-bent—excuse the expression—on wrecking the Church."

"I have a thought," said Brother Zigfried. "If His Holiness were to destroy the key, I mean publicly destroy it, they wouldn't have any reason to come after him. The Cipher would remain an encoded document forever, correct?"

"Correct, I guess. I mean, someone out there I'm sure could really go to work on it, using computers and such."

"Did he really say 'safekeeping'?"

"That's what he said," said Ridley, beginning to understand the full weight of Brother Zigfried's words.

"Then he's not going to destroy it. His Holiness is a man of his word."

"That's troublesome then," said Ridley.

"How so? Because it makes him into a target?"

"Not only that," said Ridley, "but we're doomed either way."

The Brother screwed up his face in confusion.

Ridley felt his nerves stretch almost to the breaking point. ""You don't get it. It doesn't matter who wins. Whoever wins decodes the cipher. And that spells the end for the Church."

"Then why does His Holiness hang onto it?"

"That's a question for a greater mind than mine," said Ridley. "But I do know one thing: In my darkest hour, I never thought I'd have to fight the pope."

## ROME, ITALY

"I've got a question," said Ridley. "Who was Marcion?"

Beatricia looked nervously around the cafe, then back at him.

Ridley leaned in. "You're supposed to be helping me, remember?"

"What do I get in return?" she asked. As if a mandate from the president wasn't enough.

Ridley sat back and took a breath. "I'll help you track down Mehmet's killer."

"Whoever it is, I don't want him killed."

"Understood."

"I want to do it myself," she said flatly.

He nodded. "Understood."

She breathed quietly, then brought two fingers to the bridge of her nose. She looked like she hadn't slept in days. "Marcion was considered a heretic by the early Catholic Church."

"How so?"

"Today we'd call him a Gnostic. He had a strange idea that the God of the Old Testament and the God of the New Testament were in fact two different gods. He believed that humanity was enslaved by the Old Testament God, and that Christ was delivered to this deity as a ransom for humanity."

Ridley took this in carefully. He remembered his own distaste when considering the cruelty of God in the Old Testament, and trying to square this with the gentle, peaceful God of the New.

"So," he said, "Jesus was still the Savior, just in a different way."

"It gets really strange, though. According to Gnostic beliefs, the Messiah will return as the embodiment of the eighth aeon of human history. There are thirteen aeons in all. At the eighth aeon, the Messiah will arrive."

"Can I ask when this eighth aeon is supposed to take place?"

"We're in it," she said.

"And what about the Hand of Marcion?"

"Where is Mehmet's killer?" She looked him dead in the eye.

He leaned in. "You don't get what you want until I get what I want. Do you understand?"

Her eyes narrowed contemptuously. "The Hand of Marcion is a terrorist organization headed by a man named Cyrus Knox."

"I checked out their website. Didn't get much from it. Just seemed like a bunch of mystical nonsense."

She smirked. "Don't underestimate them, Ridley. The Hand of Marcion's only desire is to hasten the return of the Messiah. They'll do it by any means necessary."

"Like how?"

Again, she narrowed her eyes, signaling contempt. "You don't see it, do you? The Shroud of Turin. An attempt on the pope's life. These aren't random attacks, Ridley. These are specific targets. And there will be more. The group was on the verge of collapse after the botched attempt on the pope's life. Cyrus Knox made some moves to solidify the loyalty of his followers. He sees himself as the Messiah."

"You're kidding."

"I wish I were."

"*That's* what's behind this?" he asked, a weak laugh escaping from his throat. "A lunatic with delusions of grandeur?"

"That's it. You were expecting something else?"

"No," he said. "It's just... I don't know. I thought there would be something... bigger. I feel like a lunatic is just pitiful. Danger-ous, but pitiful."

"He has the Nicene Cipher," she said. "He plans to usurp the pope."

"I don't understand. How?"

Beatricia explained, "He's got a lot of friends. Supporters infil-trating dioceses. The list extends into several parishes. There's one archbishop in particular. A man by the name of Centino. He hates Pope Leo like a poison. According to what I could get out of Mehmet the last time we ever spoke, Knox was planning to assassinate the pope. After the pope was out of the way, Knox would get his own man in there by gaming the system."

"But how? That takes a special conclave of Cardinals. It's a super-secret system of prayer and voting. How do they—?"

"It's very simple. You stack the conclave with your people."

"That can't be done."

"Oh no?" she said, sitting back in her chair and folding her arms. "I'm afraid our beloved Pope has already made that possi-ble. In his first year."

Ridley thought for a moment. Then the light of reason entered into him. "The edict."

Beatricia nodded slowly.

He needed to leave the cafe at once. He had to summon the Brothers.

# VATICAN CITY

Ridley paced before the group of robed monks. The scent of the damp stone walls of the cold cell did little to calm his sense of urgency.

"His Holiness is a fair and generous man," he began, then paused.

The monks looked at one another.

"Dear boy," said Brother Zigfried, "you didn't summon us here for that, did you? Because I'm afraid we were already aware."

"In his first year as pope," Ridley continued, "His Holiness issued an edict: The papal office could only appoint Cardinals every four years. Do you remember? He did it to help resist the temptation to stack the College of Cardinals with his political allies."

"The pope is well aware of the temptations that accompany power," said Brother Fernando. "He is constantly making sure the office remains uncorrupted."

"Right," said Ridley. "There's always a temptation to surround himself with a group of Cardinals who will carry on his legacy into the next papacy by voting in a likeminded pope."

The broad-chested Brother Hendrik stood up. He was an

imposing figure. "Ridley, this is a fine lesson in His Holiness's mindset. But I'm sure I speak for the rest of the group when I ask: What in the world are you talking about?"

"It's very simple," said Ridley. "I'm afraid the pope's own decency unwittingly usurped his power. By his own edict, he cannot appoint any Cardinals until next year. Before that time, the Hand of Marcion will have murdered him and placed one of their own into the office."

An incredulous laugh rose from the group. It belonged to Brother Gabriel. All heads turned.

"You can't be serious," he said. "Ridley, my friend, I think your time in the CIA has trained your mind to look for conspiracies where there are none."

"Brother Gabriel," Ridley returned, "with all due respect, I disagree."

"Well then, how do you suppose this will happen? The Hand of Marcion will corrupt the entire College of Cardinals to elect one man whom nobody has any reason to support? By what means? Coercion? This is the College of Cardinals, not a gathering of gossiping kindergarten teachers."

Ridley bit his tongue. The Brother's flippancy irked him. He calmed himself with a cleansing breath. "Brother Gabriel, the ballot is secret. All it takes is for one corrupt man to infiltrate the group. There could be a Cardinal on the payroll as we speak."

"Nonsense," said Brother Gabriel.

"Why nonsense?" retorted Brother Zigfried. "I think we should listen to Ridley."

"So, the Hand of Marcion will get their hand-selected pope. So what? What then?"

"The new pope could call an ecumenical council to institute changes to doctrine," Ridley stated plainly.

Brother Gabriel shook his head, disbelieving. "The College of Cardinals could still resist."

"Not if the College is already stacked in Knox's favor," said Ridley. "He could appoint a whole slew of yes-men Cardinals in his first year."

"Or they could already exist," said Brother Zigfried.

"What are you saying?" Brother Gabriel asked incredulously.

"I'm saying, how do we know they're not already there? How well do we really know the College? His Holiness has been a controversial figure since his election. He's loosened several Church regulations. Many aren't happy with that."

"Brother Zigfried is right," said Ridley. "And now it's time to act. I already got some information out of Beatricia Nespoli. I can get more. It's time to strike." He felt his voice rising. A power had entered him that he'd not felt since his experience in the sacristy at St. Elizabeth's.

"It's time," he declared, "to destroy the Hand of Marcion."

## TILLINGS NECK, NY

Detective Maddox entered the tiny library on Bayard Street and looked around. It smelled like old paper and was as silent as a dead office.

He headed to the reference desk. A twenty-something-year old kid was squinting at a computer screen.

"Excuse me," said Maddox.

The kid looked up. His hair was oily. He had a case of latent acne that scarred half his face.

"I called before. I'm looking for Doctor Eric Fein?"

"That's me," stated the kid.

Maddox stifled a chuckle. "What, did you just get rid of your paper route?"

The kid rolled his eyes. "I swear, I'm Eric Fein. Everyone says I look and sound younger than I am. I'm 33, actually."

Maddox rolled his tongue around his mouth. "You're the Latin expert?"

"That's right."

"Why are you working in a library?

"They got a great candy machine here," Dr. Fein said with enough snark to cut through steel.

"You're a real comedian."

The doctor took an annoyed breath. "I work at the university. I have... some debts that I need to take care of. This is only temporary."

"Huh."

"What can I do for you?"

Maddox took a piece of paper from his pocket. "I need you to translate this for me."

The youthful professor took the paper and squinted at it, mumbling the words: *"Dux fugiens haveris zelotypos karus sic quam."* He mumbled unintelligibly for a moment before saying, "This is all in the wrong order. Hang on."

He grabbed a pen from off the computer keyboard and began scribbling furiously under Maddox's scrawl, mumbling to match the pace of his pen.

"Alright, here you go," he said at last. *"Sic fugiens, dux, zelotypos, quam Karus haberis."*

"Can you translate it?"

"Yeah. *Thus fleeing, O leader, you are regarded with jealousy like Karus.*"

"OK. And does that have any significance to you?"

"Nope. Not the English anyway. It's sort of nonsense. I mean, Karus refers to the Roman Emperor Carus, with a C, rendered into Greek form."

"OK."

The kid doctor sighed impatiently. "The Latin phrase you gave me is known as a pangram."

"What's that?"

"A pangram. It's like, 'The quick brown fox jumps over the lazy dog'. It's a phrase that uses every letter of the alphabet at least once. Look. See here?" He stood up and leaned over the desk, thrusting the paper under Maddox's nose. "You can see in the Latin phrase how every letter is used. They had to borrow K, Y, and Z from the Greek to round it out and have it make sense. And of course, there's no J, V, or W because Latin doesn't use those at all."

"Of course," said Maddox.

There was a moment of silence while Maddox stared at the paper.

"Anything else?"

"Excuse me?"

"Anything else I can help you with?"

"Oh, no, it's alright. Why do people make these anyway? Pangrams?"

The kid doctor shrugged his bony shoulders. "Cuz they can."

Maddox scratched his head. "Thanks." He looked up. "Doctor."

Fein smiled appreciatively.

Maddox walked silently out of the library, running the mystery over in his head.

What could a guy like Jofar Aslan want with a Latin word gimmick?

And why the hell was it written in a damn church?

His cell phone beeped with a text message. It was his wife.

"BABY COMING."

All thoughts of Aslan went screeching out of his brain, leaving rubber and smoke behind him in a wake of heated panic, elation, and, not least of all, love.

# ROME, ITALY

Two texts. That's all it took.

He texted Beatricia about where to find Cyrus Knox. She gave him the address of a meat packaging plant.

Then a second text from her: "Good luck. He's well insulated."

Poor woman. She didn't know Ridley Shane.

It had taken a mere twenty-four hours to procure the necessary equipment. The president had been most accommodating.

A priceless assortment of the most advanced surveillance gear lay before him, neatly housed in foam rubber-lined containers.

Ridley chose Brother Hendrik to accompany him. This technical mission called for small-team secrecy. Brother Hendrik's bodybuilder frame would be more than adequate to compensate for the loss of manpower.

They left just after midnight.

The meat packaging plant was well-lit and sat recessed within a ring of barbed wire topped fencing. Brother Hendrik's wire cutters made short work of it. He was about to crawl through when Ridley stopped him.

"Hang on." Ridley scoured the ground. He spotted a softball-sized rock embedded in the dirt. It took a moment to pry loose.

He hefted it through the cut hole as far as he could. It landed, rolled a short distance, and then did exactly what he expected it to do: nothing.

"OK," he said, reassured. "Guess they don't have any motion-activated alarms."

"Unless they're silent," said Hendrik.

Ridley shot him a glance. "You have to be a downer, don't you?" He thought for a moment. "Well, I guess we just pray that no one's manning the security monitors at the moment."

With this, he crawled through.

---

THE MEN MADE their way across an untended field of grass, until they reached the concrete perimeter of the plant. The place was lit up like Times Square. The men hit the ground on their bellies.

Ridley focused his vision on the roof of the building. "I don't believe what I'm seeing."

Brother Hendrik looked for a moment, then nodded slowly. "Yeah, that's a guard on patrol, alright. And he's carrying."

"Who has an armed guard patrolling the roof of a meat packaging plant?" Ridley looked at the monk. "Unless he's got cataracts, we're in trouble." He looked around, thinking fast. "I've got an idea. First, let's get out of the light."

The men belly-crawled all the way out of the well-lit field until they were just over the eastern perimeter of the plant.

Ridley took out his phone and began texting feverishly.

"What are you doing?"

"Texting Brother Zigfried. He's got connections around town. I'm gonna see what he can do about the power grid feeding this place."

"Fifty bucks says they have a backup generator," said Brother Hendrik.

"Yeah, but I'm willing to bet we can at least get over to the building by the time it kicks in."

The men watched the guard pace across the roof.

"How much do you think they pay him?" said Brother Hendrik.

"No idea. Some gig though."

"Hey," said Hendrick, "what's with you and that Beatrice girl?"

"Beatricia. What do you mean?"

"You gonna ask her out?"

"What? No! What the hell are you talking about?"

"Nothing," Hendrik said with a shrug. "I just thought, you know, the way you look when you talk about her."

Ridley propped himself on an elbow and looked at the monk. "And how do I look when I talk about her?"

"Listen, I didn't mean anything. Let's just drop it."

"Alright," said Ridley, dropping down again and refocusing on the guard.

"Is she pretty?"

"Listen," said Ridley, "why don't *you* ask her out?"

"Hey, come on, I kinda took an oath, remember?"

"Yeah, I know. I did once. Long time ago."

"How'd you do?"

Ridley turned to him again. "Now what the hell kind of question is *that*?"

"I just happen to know it affects different people differently."

Ridley shook his head. "I prayed a lot."

Hendrik chuckled silently.

And that's when every light went out. Total darkness swallowed them instantly.

Ridley's veins buzzed with adrenaline as he got ready to book it across the field. "Cover me," he said. He steeled himself. Do or die. Preferably do. Then he moved.

With darkness serving as temporary concealment, he sprinted toward the concrete foundation of the actual building proper.

He made it to the side of the wall, out of sight of the roof guard. Fumbling like crazy, he cursed himself for his decision not to bring a larger team. He would have felt a little better having more coverage.

The emergency generators kicked in then, and the field was re-lit as if by candles. The lights weren't as bright as before, and that was a plus. But the guard would now be a tad more alert, and that was a mammoth-sized minus. That thought injected a dose of quick-dry cement into his veins.

"Come on, Shane, dammit!" he muttered, squatting to reach a spot as low on the wall as he could. He withdrew the handheld tungsten drill—another gift from the president's people—and revved it a couple of times before pressing it against the concrete wall. With his free hand, he withdrew a pistol. Be prepared, as the Scouts say.

He withdrew the drill, inserted the wireless microphone, and covered the hole with a layer of putty.

Now, he merely had the eerie amber glow of emergency lighting for coverage. He dropped to the ground and belly-crawled his way back to where Brother Hendrik lay in wait.

"What took you so long?" the monk challenged.

"I didn't realize you were a comedian," Ridley returned. "Can we get out this way?"

"Pretty sure we can."

And the men receded into the layer of woods that grew thickly behind them. And back to safety.

*Relative* safety.

He sat one pew behind Beatricia Nespoli, who sat with her head bowed, a string of rosary beads hanging from her fist.

Her hand rose over her shoulder. She was offering something. A small pendant attached to a chain. He took it and turned it around, studying it.

It was a disc with eight spokes, like a wheel with no rim. In the center of the axle was the letter S tilted about 45 degrees.

"Interesting," he said.

"It was a gift from Mehmet." There was a soft smile in her voice. "The only piece of jewelry he ever bought for me."

"What is it?"

"It's known as the Serpent Wheel," she said softly. "An emblem denoting the cycles of time until..."

Ridley leaned forward. "Until what?"

"Until the arrival of the Messiah," she said. She turned around to face him. "Ridley, I don't think you appreciate the severity of the situation."

"What's that supposed to mean?"

"They are zealots, Ridley. Right down to the last man.

Convinced that the god of the Savior is on their side. Men are dangerous when their souls are committed to this sort of bidding. They're blinded with rage and the will to assert their allegiance."

"They don't know who they're up against," he said.

"Listen, Ridley—"

"No, *you* listen. I'm tired."

"Tired of what?"

"Tired of corruption. Tired of false prophets. Tired of being a slave to a god who isn't there. I'm tired of *all of it*. I'm sorry, but I am going to fight these people. I don't care what you say. I'm not who you think I am." A well of tears grew, and his vision grew cloudy.

She was no longer Beatricia Nespoli. She was Anna Shane, back from the dead.

"Ridley," she spoke softly, "are you OK?"

"I'm sorry I killed you," he said. "I abandoned God and I killed you. I can't do it again."

He let go to the tears and the rage and ages of *my god, Anna, where are you? Where is your smile?*

"Ridley," she whispered, "you didn't kill me."

She was Beatricia Nespoli again.

"I abandoned God once..." he started.

She rose from her pew, the beads still dangling from her hand. She came around and sidestepped in next to him. And she sat down and slid over until their legs touched. Then she took his hand in hers and brought it to her mouth, placing a gentle kiss on the back of it.

She wrapped her fingers in his. They sat.

And they prayed.

# LONDON, ENGLAND

Cardinal James Madigan felt the twinge of nerves in his gut as he entered the conference hall. Jet lag made it worse. Plus, the British weather was living up to its reputation. He would have given anything to be back in L.A., basking in the sun, enjoying God's design under more comforting pretenses. Being a believer was much easier, he'd joked privately, in sunny climates.

Now he despaired, getting out of the thick air of London and entering into a grayish brown room with floors of mucked tile and metal chairs. A cardboard staleness of forced fake breeze was coming through the vents. And then there was that tinge of nerves.

It came to him whenever he found himself in a room full of religious authorities. And here he was, a religious authority.

*I'm no authority,* he thought. *I've pulled the wool over their eyes. Every damned one of them.*

But if that was true, why the fear?

Because someone *had* to know he was really a heathen masquerading as a holy man. He was certain he wore his doubt like a bad smell.

He couldn't pinpoint when it had actually happened, the

doubt. It had sort of *descended* on him, like dry dust in a room without a breeze. It had been sometime in the interim of his appointment to bishop and his subsequent appointment to cardinal by Pope Leo. And it was in the middle of his prayer before dinner, of all times.

———————

IT WAS a prayer he knew in Italian, Spanish, French, German, Dutch, Greek, and Latin, as well as English. He said it when he dined with others and when he dined alone. It was during one of the latter times that he first noticed the descent of doubt cast upon him. He had suddenly felt insignificant. His father had taught him that God was always there, and that He knew what was in our hearts. And when you said Grace, it was a marriage of two spiritual acts: Eating and praying. We take in food to continue life. And all life was for the glory of God.

But that one night when he stared down at a reheated can of Campbell's Chunky Beef and Barley soup, a glass of not-so-fine wine, and Jeopardy on the TV, something interesting and mundane and significant all at once had occurred. He picked up his spoon and couldn't remember whether or not he'd said the prayer. He sat there frozen, staring at the semi-warm mini life rafts of mystery meat, trying to recall any part of the last thirty seconds of his life. Alex Trebeck was saying something about each answer beginning with the letter 'U'. And Cardinal James Madigan stared at his soup, muttering the first words of the prayer to see if any part of it felt like déjà vu.

He wasn't depressed by it, nor was he completely befuddled. He'd suffered memory lapses before. Like when dressing, not being able to remember putting on his socks, and yet there they were on his feet.

But this wasn't socks.

He put down his spoon and bowed his head, saying the prayer again. And he felt as if he could say it a hundred times over, but the prayer was like a wrung-out sponge. There was nothing in it but syllables. Greek, Latin, English, German – it didn't matter anymore.

It frightened him.

Because he felt as if he alone had been granted a secret. The Grace prayer had been reduced to banality, like saying 'Bless you' when someone sneezed. Did anyone actually mean it in *that way*? And so the next time he walked into a room full of believers, he felt soiled. And felt like a hypocrite spewing vile gossip.

---

IT WAS ten times worse in a room full of Cardinals, like he was now.

He'd gotten the fear on the day he'd received the letter of invitation to the conference. His mind set into overdrive dreaming up an excuse not to attend. Back problems. Influenza. Plague.

*I regret to inform you that I will not be attending the conference due to a severe inflammation of the agnostic glands.*

In the end, however, he knew he must attend. He'd witnessed firsthand the strange ways in which the Lord moved, to quote another of his dreaded banalities. If he attended the conference, perhaps God would reveal himself the same way He did when James Madigan was a young seminary student. The call had been thunderous and overpowering.

Perhaps it would happen again. What was it that Yogi Berra once said? "When you come to a fork in the road, take it."

He read that many of Yogi's greatest quotes weren't actually said by the famous ballplayer. Maybe that had been the beginning of his doubt. If Yogi could be misquoted, why not Jesus? For all he knew, the Savior could have been extolling the virtues of selling counterfeit wool: *Blessed are the fleece fakers.*

His nerves relaxed when he saw the buffet table in the back of the room. He made a beeline for it. Since he was a kid, he'd buried his feelings with food. To see the piles of pastries and the coffee flowing like a mountain spring was a balm to his soul.

On the way, he was recognized by an acquaintance, Cardinal Ricardo Stelleno of Naples, who called out his name in a hearty tenor.

"How are you, my friend?" The man's English was nearly flawless, save for a curious extra vowel before or after certain words, a detail that made him sound suspiciously like Chico Marx.

"Cardinal Stelleno," he said, receiving the man's gentle hands on his shoulders and bracing himself for the European double kiss.

"Ricardo, Ricardo! I don't allow my bridge partners to call me Cardinal, why should I allow my friends to do it, eh?"

Madigan helped himself to a dense pastry that could have doubled as a paperweight.

"You like the food, eh?" He smiled warmly and knowingly.

"I should be careful not to drop it on my foot."

The man let out a raucous laugh. "Ay," he said, his laughter subsiding quickly, "tell me now whatd'ya think of the conference?"

"I'm not sure," said Madigan. The nerves in his stomach flared, and he bit into the pastry, a pocket-type thing filled with a kind of oily cream that had never once seen the inside of a cow.

"You notice who's here?"

Madigan surveyed the crowd. He recognized some of the faces, but couldn't place the names for anything.

"I recognize some," he confessed.

"Nah, nah. You know why they are here?"

Madigan shook his head, taking another tough bite.

Stelleno leaned in. "We are all *his* men."

Madigan rushed a chunk of pastry to his cheek. "Whose men?"

"Pope Leo." Stelleno said it as if it were the most obvious thing in the world. "Look around. Everyone here is pro-Leo. I am. I know you are. I know everybody is."

"OK."

"You no think that's strange?"

Madigan shrugged. "This pope has been divisive. We know that. And this conference is about anticipating doctrinal changes and how to enforce them should they arise. I guess part of dealing with them means dealing with His Holiness's opposition. I'm OK with that. I think it's time to strategize."

It was all business to Madigan. He could talk the talk just as well as anyone in the room. What was in his heart, however...

"Me," said Stelleno, "I don't believe it. I think it's a, whatd'ya call, a *ruse*."

"Explain."

The Italian Cardinal shrugged. "Eh, maybe I'm wrong. All this talk about doctrine. It's leading us away from the topics we need to discuss."

The lights blinked twice.

"Looks like they're starting. Bring your coffee and doorstop."

He smiled at his acquaintance and carried his coffee and his miserable pastry over to a seat on the aisle, toward the back of the room.

It was right about this time that Madigan noticed what was truly odd about the room. True, most if not all of the men here were allies of the pope. They were all *young*. He was used to periodic gatherings of the College of Cardinals where the age range ran the gamut from middle-aged and distinguished to old and falling apart at the seams. Here, it was only the former.

He turned his attention to the lectern at the front of the

room. Murmurings around him sunk to a mellow sound of patient waiting, then rose to impatience, then died down again.

No one approached the lectern. Madigan caught bits of stifled questions – a word here, an inflection there – from the men around him.

He brought his pastry to his lips for a bite. It smelled sickly sweet. Like camphor.

He brought it closer. It wasn't the pastry. A breeze struck him. And the next thought was one of mild relief that they'd turned on the air in here. But the smell, now sharp and acrid, entered his sinuses like a needle.

Men around him began to cough and wheeze and gasp.

Several got up. The murmur rose in intensity to a panicked scramble of words and coughs and heaves.

Madigan stood up. He brought the front of his robe up over his nose, copying the actions of several men who were making their way to the exit.

And then, music. He recognized it immediately in the chaotic whirl of panicked Cardinals, all of whom were now up and heading toward the double doors of the room's only egress.

The piece was the 1812 Overture. The cannons blasted, the triumphant strings and deep, resonant horns blared and scraped in triumphant glory.

And men began to drop.

Cardinal James Madigan's coffee and pastry were on the floor, and he was on his knees. Although he was no atheist in this foxhole, he wasn't in this position because of prayer. His leg muscles had simply given out.

His lungs seared like they'd been doused with fire. The music was loud and intense. The few who made it to the door thrust their flat palms against it, their anguished cries drowned out by the strains of Tchaikovsky.

Madigan's eyes blurred with hot tears. He gasped. Then his nose hit the floor.

Exactly one minute later, fifty men lay dead in the room.

# VATICAN CITY

"Good news," said Brother Hendrik upon entering the common room, "we've got intel."

Ridley stiffened at the sound of the monk's voice. He'd been trying his hand at a bit of meditation. Something about this place lent itself well to that particular distraction.

"Oh," said the monk, "sorry, friend."

"It's alright."

"Normally I'd allow you to continue," Brother Hendrik said with a trace of apology in his voice, "but this is important."

What little meditation Ridley had completed allowed him to accept the interruption with a modicum of charity. "Go on," he said.

"It seems our friend Knox is planning to ditch the cipher."

"Where?"

The monk shook his head. "You won't believe it."

"Try me."

"The Fontanelle crypts."

"In Naples?"

The monk nodded.

"Odd choice."

"Not so odd," said Brother Hendrik. "Knox has a contact there. A security guard. He's paid the man off and will slip in tomorrow night around midnight."

Ridley smirked. "Midnight in the crypts, huh?"

"Should be an adventure."

Ridley stood up, feeling a lightness in his body thanks to the meditation. "Alrighty," he said with a cleansing breath, "let's go tell the others. We don't have much time."

RIDLEY WAS TURNING over plans for a possible ambush, and Brother Hendrik was still mentally scrutinizing the chatter picked up by their well-placed, ultra-sensitive, pinpoint adjustable focus microphone courtesy of the CIA. But neither man was prepared for the sight that greeted them when they entered the papal office.

The pope sat gravely at his desk, his fingers tented before him. The men sat around in a semi-circle, some with heads bowed. The most disconcerting thing to Ridley was the fact that not one person picked their head up to acknowledge either one of the new entrants.

"Is everything alright?" said Ridley, his voice heavy in the room.

The room was a still photo animated for a few frames, as heads rose from clasped hands, and the pope's eyes shifted their way.

"Where were you?" demanded Brother Aaron.

"I was... in contemplation," said Ridley, substituting a word with less Eastern mystic connotations.

"And I was analyzing the surveillance chatter."

The pope inhaled audibly, his head swiveling slowly throughout the room.

The Brothers were aware of this as a sign of reticence on the pope's behalf. Brother Aaron spoke again.

"There's been... an event."

"What kind of event?" asked Ridley.

"A meeting of the College of Cardinals," continued Brother Aaron, "was convened at a hotel in the U.K."

"Not on my authorization," said the pope, his fierce voice snapping all heads in his direction.

Brother Aaron swallowed hard. "Not on His Holiness's authorization. The entire group was murdered. Poisoned by gas."

"I don't understand," said Brother Hendrik.

Brother Aaron began to speak but was stifled at the sound of the pope clearing his throat.

"The murdered men," said Pope Leo, slowly and with great articulation, "did not comprise the whole of the College of Cardinals. They were a select group of fifty men who were sympathetic to me. Someone summoned them to that place with the express purpose of killing them."

"Dear God," muttered Ridley. He rubbed his face with his hand, then looked up to see the pope glaring directly at him.

"What do you think this means?" inquired His Holiness.

"What do *I* think?" asked Ridley. He had the impression that the man knew the answer, but was testing him. After a moment, he said, "I think, Your Eminence, that someone wants to replace you. I think your life is in danger. I think whoever is responsible for this will kill you. And I think this... this massacre... ensures that you will not be replaced by someone like you."

The pope nodded once, never taking his eyes off Ridley.

"There will be a coup on the Catholic Church," said Ridley. He felt a strange power in his voice. No longer was he running from a fear, but turning to face it. For this was the burning truth of his nightmares, the rendering of his faith from top to bottom, like the sanctuary curtain in the New Testament, and the spilling out of its guts upon the floor.

"The Church will die," said the pope, now turning to face every man in the room. "I have met with Beatricia Nespoli."

The mere mention of the name ignited a hot current of nerves in Ridley's stomach. How did the man know about Beatricia?

"I see your confusion," Pope Leo said to Ridley. "In a fit of doubt, I contacted President Zimmer. He directed me to Signora Nespoli. And she explained to me exactly what is at stake."

He rose from his desk slowly. Not a sound was made as he came from around it and paced among the men, speaking ethereally, as though he were addressing someone in another dimension of space.

"The Nicene Cipher is a terrible thing. It is a sacrilege. Added to official doctrine, our Church will be obliterated, replaced by a heresy. And with this new doctrine will be born a schism such as the world has never seen. Because of the nature of those who will see it to its end, there will be terrible violence. Brother will turn against brother. We will see a new inquisition, a new crusade, and bloodshed in the name of Christ. There is enough of that in the world already, no? Brothers, our personal faith is strong. It is eternal. Should the Church be destroyed, we have the truth in our hearts, and that is enough for the Lord. But what becomes of the flock when the master is struck, eh?"

He stopped before Ridley and turned to him. His eyes smoldered. "Are you prepared now?"

Ridley understood what he meant. Prepared: spiritually, physically, and tactically.

"I am."

The pope smiled ironically. "You use the words of the Father when he spoke to Moses. You understand the implications then?"

"I do," replied Ridley, his voice slightly tremulous.

"Tell the others."

"We're preserving not only our own faith by defeating these people, but the faith of our Jewish and Muslim brothers as well. For if one falls, they all do."

Pope Leo nodded and walked back to his desk. "The differing faiths of these three peoples are responsible for much conflict and strife on earth, and not one is innocent of sins against humanity. But they are, each and every one of them, People of the Book, and must be respected and nurtured. I'm afraid our opponents think otherwise."

"Holy war," said Ridley. "That's what you meant. Not among ourselves. Not to compete. But to fight a common enemy."

"It is you who have said it," said the pope.

"We have intel," said Ridley. "Knox is going to attempt to place the Nicene Cipher somewhere within the crypts at Fontanelle tomorrow night. We ought to be ready for them."

There was once again a dreadful silence in the room. Ridley quickly assessed what it was due to: they were all waiting for the go-ahead from the man behind the desk.

Their leader sat down with the air of a man content with having made a resolution. A good resolution or a bad one; it didn't matter. It was enough that there was a defined goal.

"Go with God," the pope said quietly.

# ROME, ITALY

A flickering fire threw the shadow of Cyrus Knox on the wall as he paced. He stayed as far from the fireplace as he could; the stuffiness in the room, already packed beyond fire code capacity, was soon going to be unbearable.

As he paced, he stole glances of the group of men and women who were gathered together in his home office, huddled close like prisoners on a chain gang. All were glistening with sweat.

*Just a minute more,* he thought. He wanted to feel the discomfort wafting off them for just one minute more.

When the heat in the room became unbearable, he spoke.

"A friend once told me he had a dog who kept doing his business on the carpet. You know what he did? He got rid of the carpet. Did the problem go away? I'll give you eighteen guesses."

A tide of nervous laughter came forward, then receded.

"No," he continued, "The problem lay with the dog. Take a look at all the nastiness in the world. All the evil. Is that the work of man? My friends, we did not ask to be created this way. The fault lies with the manufacturer."

Again, the laughter came, this time in a small trickle forward.

"The    Creator    God    is    the    problem,    and    only    the

Redeemer can take us forward to our true destiny. Is there anyone here who denies this?" He turned, making eye contact with each person one at a time. "Anyone here still hold to that idiot notion of one God, one Son, and all that? A father who creates us sick and then commands us to be well?"

Each man and woman's breathing increased. The heat, the stuffiness, the intensity of his voice – it all worked to his benefit. He felt himself getting aroused at the prospect.

"On earth, as it is in heaven," he said, bowing his head. "The current pope of the Catholic Church is a weak-willed rodent, making it up as he goes along. Look at the morality of the world. I ask you, is this effective?"

Again, he looked from eye to eye. With each contact, a breathy acknowledgment from the person.

"When you look at the state of the world, I say it's like looking at that carpet. It's not the rug, it's the dog. The dog must go."

Laughter, a few coughs brought on by the heat and airlessness, and someone said, "Hear, hear!"

Knox sauntered over to his right. He approached a gentleman in a dark suit who sat stone-faced in a club chair in the corner of the room. He held out his hand and the man rose. Knox took it and gently guided the man closer. Knox then put an arm around him.

"My friends, I looked long and hard for this man. The Father of our Redeemer brought him into my life. This man," he turned and beamed at the man like a proud papa, "this man shall be his gatekeeper. I give you, Father Severn."

The room erupted into sycophantic applause. Father Severn held up both hands for silence.

"Thank you, friends." He spoke in a thick, buttery Southern accent. "We've faced dark days in recent times, but I assure you, that time is comin' to an end. Just a few days ago, a gatherin' of Cardinals was held in a hall in the United Kingdom."

*Yoo-notted Kingdom.*

"Fifty men entered that hall. And fifty men were called to their reward."

He paused for effect, as Knox stood by his side, staring down the faces of his subjects.

"Every one of those men stood between us and the papacy. And now all that is left for us is to fulfill our moral obligation to the world and ascend to the highest office on this blessed earth, friends. I shall be elected pope, fair and square, when the time comes. And I will be your shepherd."

A smattering of applause began, hesitantly, and then grew into a hearty round.

Knox stepped forward. "Yes, my friends, that is how we roll here in Catholic town. We have done away with every obstacle but one, and that one is not long for this world. Pope Leo... is a marked man."

He smiled lugubriously as the applause grew and bounced off the walls of the tiny, stuffed office.

"And now," said Knox, "I saved the best news for last. As you may or may not have heard, one of our own was killed in America. He was after the key to the Nicene Cipher, which lay in a small church in New York. He died for our cause, and so is to be honored as a martyr. This is indeed a happy occasion, for all who go to their death for me are to be glorified, and so they glorify us all by being counted among our numbers." He paused to pick a small glass of wine off his desk. "I will drink this fine port to his memory. And I ask you all to do the same."

At this moment, the door to the office opened, and light and cool air rushed in. A woman stepped in holding a tray of similar glasses filled halfway with ruby port.

The men took their glasses. Some with trepidation. Knox

watched who they were that hesitated, and let his eyes linger on them.

He held up his glass and bowed his head. "Father of the Redeemer, I ask that you consecrate this wine, and that you let the power of your love transform it into the blood of your Son. Your light guides us and keeps us pure. We ask that the mystery of your power be withheld until that day when we need it most. So be it."

"So be it," echoed the congregation.

Knox smiled, and drank.

He watched them.

"OK," he said jovially as he set the glass down on the desk. "Let's have a little fun tonight, shall we? We've arranged for a screening of the original *King Kong*. I love that movie. Always have." He clapped his hands together. "Brother Richard, you still have that stash of popcorn? Or did your wife use it all up watching your wedding video again?"

A sprinkling of chuckles.

"Come on," said Knox. "What's with all the lifeless faces? Ain't they got lifeless faces, Father?" He looked over at Father Severn.

"I coulda told them they all won the lottery just now and I bet they wouldn't change their faces."

The mood in the room lightened a bit. A muffled conversation rose to a joking tone. Several men laughed. Smaller conversations broke out.

"And let's get some damn fresh air in here," said Knox. "Is it me, or does it feel like you could bake a ham in here?"

The door opened, and the long-awaited gush of light and freshness entered.

"There we are," said Knox. "You are all dismissed. The movie's at eight. That's one hour from now. Y'all should be dead by then."

Everything slowed to a stop.

"Oh," said Knox, feigning absentmindedness, "did I forget to mention the poison?"

He looked from face to face, relishing the anguish and confusion.

The room was dead silent.

No one complained. Not one.

Knox smiled brightly, unabashed and feeling wonderful.

"Now this," he said gently, with a tremor in his voice, "this is what I want. You all drank, and when I told you what I told you, not one of you objected. This is what I wanted to see. My friends, this was a test of your loyalty. I know now... I know..." Tears streamed down his face.

"Thank you, Jesus," he said, Raising his eyes to heaven. "Thank you."

One man ran outside and threw up. Just one. The rest lowered their face to their hands and wept, silently or not, along with their beloved leader.

# LAZIO, OUTSKIRTS OF ROME, ITALY

Outside Rome, in the greater region of Lazio, is a series of tree-lined hills. Old roads cut through the hillside. If one were to speed through, they would miss the turn onto an unmarked path, barely wide enough for their Hummer.

It was down this very path that Ridley Shane and two of the Brothers of St. Longinus traveled cautiously. They had decided that at least two or three of the others should remain behind to guard Pope Leo. He had Vatican security. But the Vatican security, for all their professionalism and fortitude, were *not* the Brothers of St. Longinus.

Brother Zigfried, phone in hand, shifted his eyes from the device to the road and back again.

"Another three quarters of a mile," he said.

None of the men had spoken much at all on the journey here. The tension in the vehicle was palpable, the air thick like the smell of ozone.

"I would kill the lights now, ol' boy," said Zigfried, handing him a pair of night vision goggles.

Ridley looked over at his fellow soldier, nodded and received the goggles in hand. After donning them, he killed the headlights and downshifted the engine to keep it as soft as possible.

In the silent dark night, they had about as much chance of remaining stealthy as a rabid wolfhound let loose in a mime school. But they had to at least make *some* effort at reducing their likelihood of getting caught.

La Chiesa San Pietro Damiani seemed to spring from the surrounding vegetation up ahead on the left. It was the size of a cottage, and its facade was peeling away with nine hundred years of meteorological abuse. The chapel proper consisted of a Spanish-style portico entrance that was its only inviting feature. The rest was a medieval nightmare of a place — rectangular windows cut into the facade, giving the place a look that was more Early-American jail cell than place of worship. Behind, a bell tower rose to twice the height of the church, and had all the structural integrity of a game of Jenga nearing its finish.

"Abandon all hope, ye who enter here," muttered Ridley.

"And just think," said Zigfried, "that's just the outside. Our destination is much worse, I fear."

An SUV came into sight; it had been parked within the scruff of vegetation that grew all around the place.

"Alright, folks," said Ridley, "show time."

Zigfried turned back to Brother Aaron, who had a pair of night vision binoculars to his eyes. "Anything?"

"Nada."

Ridley pulled the Hummer past the church and cut the engine.

Each man did a quick check of his gear and stepped from the vehicle.

With the silence and stealth of hungry cats, they assumed positions outside the church, each keeping his own optimal vantage.

Zigfried's voice came in through Ridley's earpiece, clear as night. The government had paid good money for this technology. "Well now, isn't this cozy."

"Could be worse."

"Tell us how," said Aaron, "we're all waiting."

Ridley managed a strained grin. "We could be in the Amazon. They have spiders as big as your face."

"*Ecch*," said Aaron.

"You asked," said Ridley.

"He's right, dear boy."

"Why do I get the feeling we should have brought more men?" Ridley asked himself.

There was no answer from the other two, leading Ridley to believe that it was a thought that had obviously crossed their minds as well.

The waiting was excruciating, watching the front of the building for any sign of movement. The men were trained for this very sort of exercise in endurance. In fact, they prided themselves on their ability. But that didn't make the task easy.

Suddenly, a shadowy figure appeared in the doorway. Ridley braced himself. He heard the sudden intake of air come through his headset.

There, in the doorway, was Beatricia, a thick arm around her neck and a pistol to her temple. The look on her face was pure anguish.

"Help," she cried softly, "Ridley?"

"Oh my," said Zigfried.

"We didn't prepare for this," said Aaron.

"No kidding," said Ridley.

A deep male voice, heavily accented, cut through the black night. "Nobody moves."

A blinding light shone from under the portico, coming from the man's headgear.

"Rise and drop your weapons!" shouted the voice.

"Hang tight, guys," muttered Ridley, slowly and deliberately making a show of doing what the voice had told him to do. He capped it by putting both hands in the air.

"Come to me," said the voice.

"Meet me halfway."

"Nonsense."

"I'm unarmed."

"Ridley," cried Beatricia in a wavering tone, "listen to them."

"Them," repeated Brother Aaron.

"That SUV seats six at most," said Zigfried.

It was then that Ridley realized his amateur mistake: he'd left his headset on – a sure indicator that he was not alone.

A quick glance to his right told him all he needed to know. The area illuminated by the light terminated at a scruff of weeds nearly fifteen feet away. He made a dash for it and dove out of the light.

His Hail Mary move turned out to be a correct one, for the bearer of the light couldn't reach where Ridley was without coming out of the portico and becoming a target himself.

Brother Aaron fired a single shot, purposely hitting the stones behind the figure with the headlight, who dragged a squirming Beatricia forward to avoid it.

The figure backed up, turning his hostage toward Aaron's position.

"Blast," said Zigfried. "I can't get a decent shot."

"I'm gonna try to get him to turn," said Ridley, preparing to dart from the bushes.

"I don't think that's wise," said Zigfried. "You're not armed."

"Neither is he, really," said Ridley. "He's got his gun on the girl."

"Um," said Aaron, "that doesn't make much sense."

"I know what Beatricia is capable of," said Ridley. "And if he's smart, he does too. He's not going to take that gun off her for a second."

Before either man could protest any further, Ridley darted from his hiding position and charged.

He guessed right. The figure merely backed up and maneuvered his human shield directly in front of him.

"Stop!" he shouted. "I will kill her!"

"Ridley, for God's sake!" screeched Beatricia. "Stop!"

There was something pained and terrible in her voice that froze him. He could hear her panting as the man dragged her backwards, whispering raspy commands in her ear as they disappeared into the chapel.

The light on his head went off, and Ridley was plunged into darkness.

"We have to go in," Ridley said.

"That would be suicide," said Zigfried. "They knew we were coming. They had to have known. They're waiting for us."

Ridley stood powerless, clenching his fists as intense rage rose like magma from his guts.

Then an idea entered his brain.

He almost laughed. How could he have been so stupid?

"We're going in," Ridley stated. "Get ready for a fight."

"You can't be serious," said Zigfried, now coming toward him from his left. Aaron too had left his position and was joining the men.

Ridley turned to the rest of his team.

"They're not going to kill Beatricia," he said. "She's the expert they need. She knows a lot more than all of us put together. Besides, as far as they're concerned, she has the disc with the key to the cipher on it. They won't kill her until they have that."

"They'll torture her," said Brother Aaron.

Ridley looked sternly at him. "All the more reason why we have to get our asses in there. Now."

Without another word between them, the men did a quick inventory of their gear, while Ridley collected his from where he'd dropped it.

And the three men mentally readied themselves for battle.

## LAZIO, OUTSKIRTS OF ROME, ITALY

Brother Zigfried was right: inside was worse.

The place had lain in ruins for a very long time, hidden within the obscurity of an overgrown Italian countryside. The smell in here was not the smell of fresh rot, or newly-excavated tombs; rather, it was the smell of long-dead memories, of old things, of cold rocks and powdered earth. It was a chilling smell, one that gave the sense that you were inhaling the very dust of the dead themselves.

Wooden pews, rotted and crumbling, sat in waiting for the return of ancient worshippers. Whatever religious iconography that had once been here was now long gone. Pillaged perhaps, or perhaps taken up by the Almighty, so as not to allow the ravages of time to pervert them as well.

The men stepped carefully within. Ridley heard the scurry and scratching of a heavy rodent somewhere not far away from his heel, like a body being dragged across the floor. Up past the altar, he spotted an arched doorway, merely a hole in the wall without a door. As he crept toward it, it became obvious that it was a stone staircase leading downward. With extreme silence, he pressed on, motioning for the men to follow.

When they reached the arched doorway, Ridley paused for a moment. Then he entered, rifle first.

The steps wound down in a tight spiral. There was barely enough room for two people to pass. The smell here was more intense, and added to it was an odor like that of mold or ancient fungus. God knows what would be rubbing off on his sleeves as they descended.

But it wasn't the stench or the mold that bothered him, it was the silence. It was not a stillness due to the utter desolation of the place. That would have been tolerable. This was the silence of something lying in wait for his approach. Somewhere down in that thick lump of darkness was a hulking beast, perhaps nearer than he thought, breathing steadily and ready to pounce. He tightened his grip on the rifle.

The steps led them into a sort of antechamber, approximately nine by nine feet. There were Latin inscriptions on the wall, a crucifix, and an empty candle rack of rusted iron. And there were bones stacked in neat piles on either side, topped with skulls. They padded through here and found themselves in a much larger cavern. Stacked bones and skulls appeared everywhere around them in heaps. Skulls in pyramid piles. Bones littering the corners like the feasting table of cannibals.

Besides the bones of the dead, the men were alone here.

"I don't get it," said Brother Aaron. "There's no other place they could have gone."

It was true. There were no visible exits. The only way out was the way they had come.

"*Around me tread the mighty dead and slowly pass away,*" said Brother Zigfried.

Ridley looked back at him. "Lewis Carroll?"

"Very good."

"I wish it solved this little mystery."

There was a spark of light to their left.

In the nanosecond it took to process the flash, all conscious action shut off. Ridley found himself on the ground, a scattering of debris flying past his face.

Then the conscious mind began to work. An explosion. His ears were ringing from it. He was hurting. Where? In his face, of course. A vague sound of pain struck him. Not his own. One of the others. Aaron? Zigfried? Slowly, dizzily, he picked himself off the cold stone floor. The night goggles were still functional. It took him a moment to get his bearings and register what had happened.

One of the skulls, it seemed, had exploded.

The other two men got up, relatively unharmed.

Another flash and pop, this time a little further away from them. Ridley averted his night vision gaze. Bone fragments flew through the air and hit the wall opposite. Then another skull exploded near the second one.

Each blast pounded his eardrums. The closest thing Ridley could compare them to were the M80s he and his friends used to light on the Fourth of July when they were kids. And with each blast came a rain of debris. Bones and dust and pebbles.

Again and again, skulls exploded left and right.

The logical thing to do was retreat.

He was in no mood for logic. Every explosion pissed him off more than the last. Sure that first one had knocked them off their feet, but had done little to no obvious harm. It was a scare tactic, and an obnoxious one at that.

He started toward the middle of the room.

"Come on Shane!" yelled Brother Zigfried. "Dammit, boy, where's your head?"

Another blast, and another rain of bone shrapnel. He felt it cut into his face. He swore under his breath.

He made his way toward the far wall, shielding himself as best as he could with one arm, the other holding his rifle aloft, as if that would deter any further explosions.

"There's a way out somehow," he shouted, a venomous anger in his voice. "I'm gonna find it."

Another explosion, this one a little too close. He staggered a bit, then caught himself before falling. His ears throbbed from the booms.

He reached the far wall and threw himself against it. It had to give somewhere.

By this point, the other men had followed him into the middle of the room, dodging shrapnel as well.

"It's gotta be here," he rasped out.

"*Que es?*" said Aaron, reverting to Spanish under pressure.

"A latch or a hinge or something," said Ridley, pressing frantically against different sections of the wall as another detonation rained bone shards against their backs.

"Secret passages like that are only in movies!" cried Brother Zigfried, tugging at his arm. "Come on! We can't stay here!"

Ridley noticed it first. There in the corner, obscured by several stacks of bones. It was a niche cut into the wall, ostensibly for the storage of a coffin. It was close to the floor, and as Ridley moved toward it, he could tell it was empty. He leaned down and stuck his arm into it. Nothing. A giant hole. He felt the base of it and determined that it inclined steeply.

As three more deafening explosions rattled his brains, he climbed into the coffin-sized hole sideways, rolled down, and landed on a stone floor in an empty chamber.

The two men followed suit. They could hear the continued explosions tearing the charnel house to shreds. They looked around. There was a passage, similar to the arched doorway beside the altar upstairs in the church. Through the doorway were steps leading up.

He turned to his friends. They were powdered with debris and bleeding from cuts on their faces.

"You guys don't look so good," he said, his own voice slightly muffled in his ears from the noises they'd endured.

"Shall I produce a mirror for you to take in your own handsome visage?" said Brother Aaron, with a wry grin.

"I'm alright," said Ridley, brushing at his sleeves. "Let's go."

And they made their way to the steps.

At the top of the steps was a wooden door. Ridley kicked it open and the barrel of his rifle leading the way through.

He was outside the church. He looked around. No one.

He stepped out fully. The other two stepped out behind him, each one spying all directions of the compass for an ambush.

Gunfire sprayed the wall to his left. The three men scattered.

There was the roar of a car engine revving, and the spinning of tires on mud.

The vehicle sped past Ridley, showering gunfire in a chaotic splash. He dove into a tangle of weeds.

He heard the car receding. Soon the sound of the engine had faded, dissolved really, into the sounds of the night.

It was replaced by moaning. From not one, but two men.

Zigfried and Aaron were both hit.

## ROME. ITALY

"I can't believe how terrible I feel," said Ridley.

He sat in the hospital cafeteria nursing a cup of weak coffee. Brothers Aaron and Zigfried were both in intensive care, having suffered hits to the chest and stomach, respectively.

Brother Gabriel sat calmly opposite, a peaceful air about him. "You don't need to feel terrible."

"I'm responsible."

"If you feel that way, then feel sorry. Don't feel terrible. You'll chip away at your soul until there's nothing left."

"But it's my fault. They led us into a trap."

"How so?"

"They knew we bugged them," said Ridley, a tad annoyed that the monk wasn't getting it. "They obviously fed us bad intel. The oldest trick in the book, and I fell for it like a rube."

"I know they led you into a trap," said Gabriel. "I wanted to know, how is it your fault?"

Ridley put two fingers to the corners of his eyes. His facial lacerations stung from multiple bone fragments. The topical anesthetic they gave him was beginning to wear off. Gabriel had met him at the hospital just as they were releasing him. Coffee had seemed like a good idea then. Now, he just wanted to stick his face into a tub of iced aloe and sleep for five days.

"It was my idea," he said. "My idea to bug them. My idea to follow up on the scoop we got from the bug. My idea not to retreat."

"What would have happened had you retreated?"

"God knows."

"Exactly."

"What's your point?" Ridley was ready to get up and leave. Only his reverence for the monk kept him seated.

The monk sat back and smiled. "What about your nightmares?"

"What about them?"

"Have they subsided?"

Ridley stared at the table and licked his lips. "No."

Brother Gabriel let out a soft chuckle through his nose.

Ridley looked up. "What's so funny?" The monk had a grin on his face.

"Sitting opposite me," Brother Gabriel said in a lighthearted tone, "is this six-foot-one, cleanly baldheaded man. An imposing figure with a stare that could freeze the sun. And yet," he leaned forward, hands on the table, "inside him is a heart that rages against injustice and carries the cross for his friends. That, my friend, is what is so funny. You are a walking contradiction. So tough on the outside. On the inside, enough spiritual fire to burn the world and then some."

"I'm done with this," Ridley said plainly.

"I'm sorry?"

"I said I'm done. Tell His Holiness I am going to resign from the mission. Everything I've done so far has wound up in disaster. He has the key to the cipher. Without that, Knox and his disciples can't do much."

"You're forgetting that they are guilty of mass murder. The

cardinals..."

"Yes, and that's our fault too."

"Come again?"

"Listen, has it occurred to you that maybe this is God's plan after all? Maybe we're meant to lose. Name me one battle in history where one side did not believe they were backed by the Almighty. Oh no," he leaned back and waved his hand, "thank you, I'm out. It's become clear that I jumped into a fight that I'm not meant to win."

The monk was silent for some time. Then he said, "I'm very sorry to hear this."

Something caught Ridley's eye in his peripheral vision. He looked up. Pope Leo was walking toward their table.

Both men stood up immediately. It was then that Ridley realized that they were the only ones in the cafeteria. The pope had been preceded by a bodyguard, who, along with a half a dozen others, now stood watch at the opening to the cafeteria.

"I told them I was visiting a friend," Pope Leo said kindly, his arms open and inviting. "Your cover isn't blown."

"Your Eminence," said Ridley, moving to take his hand for a kiss.

"No, no, please," said the pope. "Recover first. Besides, remember John the Baptist when he met Our Lord at the Sea of Galilee. It is I who should greet you in such a manner."

Brother Gabriel looked at Ridley. "Now is your chance."

Ridley lowered his head. "Your Holiness," he said with half a voice, "I'm sick at heart. My actions have possibly cost us the lives of two men. Who knows how many more will die or be hurt, or worse – who knows if we'll succeed? I can't stay here any longer. I'm going back to the States."

The pope drew a breath, his back straightening as he did. "You've prayed on this?"

Ridley felt embarrassed to answer. "Not exactly."

The pope nodded his head silently. He then turned to Brother Gabriel. "Would you excuse us?"

"Of course, Your Eminence."

Brother Gabriel left the cafeteria. The pope motioned to the table where they'd been sitting. "Please."

Ridley retook a seat, and the pope sat opposite. It was a surreal sight to say the least, this holy man in full garb filling out a cheap seat at a cheap table in a hospital cafeteria.

"I've turned from God," Ridley said quietly, his voice wavering.

"And what? You're afraid He won't be there when you return?"

Ridley shook his head. "It isn't that. It's just... I'm not up to this task."

The pope nodded. "Yes, and Moses was a powerful soldier; no, a king, when he was called."

Ridley couldn't smile at the man's levity.

"No one is up to the task that He calls us to. But He calls us because it is in his grand design. He has set the stage, and we are His players."

Ridley now recalled his recurring nightmare.

"I see it in your face," said the pope.

Ridley looked up.

"The stage," said the holy man. "Brother Gabriel told me of your dream. You are afraid that the two sides of life, good and evil, those which war for our souls, will engulf you in the conflict."

"Not me, Your Eminence, others."

"And so you feel their souls are your responsibility?"

"Your Eminence," said Ridley, his voice having returned fully to him, "a moment ago you asked me if I'd prayed. I was truthful and I told you no. But the truth is, I think I made up my mind to walk away from this the first night I ever had that dream. What if that's God's way of telling me I'm not prepared for it? What then? Am I to disobey?"

Pope Leo rose from the table. "No, son. You shouldn't disobey."

Ridley bowed his head. "I'm sorry."

"I know," the pope said. There was more than a trace of sadness that nearly broke Ridley's heart to hear.

"I will get someone else more capable," said Ridley. "I'll talk to the president. We'll get Daniel, or my friend Cal. They've got a team of men more than capable of assisting you and the Brothers."

The pope bowed his head. "OK. Go and rest, son." He stepped closer, put his hand on Ridley's head and closed his eyes, muttering a prayer in Latin. His touch was warm and soft and dry.

And strong.

Ridley closed his eyes and felt a tear run down his cheek. He couldn't help it.

When he opened his eyes, the pope was already walking away, the bodyguards having closed like seawater around his receding form.

HE FELT anything but relief as he filled his suitcase with the clothes from his hotel room drawers. Some ibuprofen had done the trick to soothe his stinging face. It was seven in the morning. He hadn't slept. He wanted to wake up to the relief of packing his bags and getting ready to leave this place.

It was going to take some time to live this one down. He was ready for it. It was the right decision when you factored in all that had gone wrong.

His cell phone rang. He looked at it and saw a number he didn't recognized. The area code and the ID told him it was New York calling.

"Hello?"

"Is this Ridley Shane?"

"Speaking."

"Yeah," said the man's voice. "I hope I'm not calling too early. It's one in the morning here."

"Who is this?"

"This is Detective Maddox from the Tillings Neck Police Department in New York. I've made a bunch of phone calls and they led me to you. I'm sure hoping you can help, because, let me tell ya, I'm a little over my head here. My wife just had a baby, you know. Anyway, that's neither here nor there. Have you got a minute, Mr. Shane?"

"Uh, yeah, I suppose."

"Oh, great. Seriously, cuz like I said, this thing is a little beyond me at the moment. You see, we had a homicide here and yours truly is having a heck of a time trying to figure it all out. Can I run a few things by you?"

"Sure."

"OK, well, let me just start by saying this: Do you know a certain Virginia Salinger?"

Ridley thumbed through his mental phone book. "Doesn't ring a bell."

"Huh. Well, you see, this is where I get stuck too. Let me back up a bit. So, we have this homicide here a couple of weeks ago. Guy by the name of Jofar Aslan. Does, uh, does *that* name ring a bell by any chance?"

"Aslan? As a matter of fact, it does."

"Yeah," said the detective, "I thought it might. Anyway, this guy Aslan gets gunned down in a drive-by. Turns out, he's got no friends or family anywhere except in Europe: one brother, a guy named Mehmet."

"That's right," said Ridley.

"Glad to hear you know him. It took a while to get that info, you see. I wasn't working that part of the case. And when the info came in, I was on leave. My wife gave birth to a six and a half pound baby boy."

"Congratulations," Ridley murmured.

"Aw, thank you. Thank you very much. But the point is, I was out for that, and you know when you're off of work for a while and you come back to a shit show? Cuz no one knows how to take care of business while you're gone?"

"I guess I know what you mean."

"Yeah? Well, that's what happened. It kinda makes a guy feel good about himself. You know, the place would crumble without ya. It sure does pile on the work. But I got to it, you know? And I took this new evidence and combined and correlated it with my own. And here's where it starts to get interesting. This guy Jofar was shot while standing out in front of a church here in town. It was bothering me. I asked myself, 'What was he doing there?' I went inside the church, and I think I may have found it. Strange stuff, I'll tell ya. But I'll get to that in a moment. Let me go back to the things I found out after I came back in to work. I needed more info on this guy Mehmet, since he was the only living relative, as far as we knew. We found his name on a lease for an apartment in Turkey. But while digging there – and here's the strange part – we find out that the credit card he used was issued under a different name: *Elia Price-Bastino*. What's odd about that name?"

"Nothing I can think of at the moment."

"I felt the same way first time around. But then I remembered something. Among the evidence found at the scene of Jofar's murder was a book. And scrawled in the margin on one of the pages was a notation, a bizarre phrase: *Polite arabs in ice*."

Ridley thought for a moment. "An anagram?"

Detective Maddox sounded surprised. "Bingo, my friend. Now, if you were me, you'd have a little mystery to solve. You'd have a name and a phrase that's an anagram of it. Or, is it the other way around? That's the mystery I had on my hands. So, I dug some more into the owner of that credit card. Would you believe I came up short?"

"Actually, I would," said Ridley, reclining and closing his eyes the way he would while listening to music.

"Smart man. There is no Elia Price-Bastino. Oh, there are a few records with that name on them – credit cards and such – but that's it. So we researched them all. Know what we found?"

"I haven't a clue."

"Smart man again. Never speculate. It's dangerous in my profession. One of the credit cards we found had a plane ticket charged to it. A ticket to America. To LaGuardia Airport. My neck of the woods. And his brother's, in case you haven't guessed."

"Paying for a plane ticket with a made-up identity?" said Ridley. "Isn't that a little...?"

"A little nervy in this day and age? Yes, yes it is. Kinda makes you think the guy was up to no good, doesn't it?"

"I would say so."

"So now," said Maddox, "we got a dead guy here in America, and across the ocean is his brother who's travelling to America under an assumed name. Right?"

"Right."

There was silence for a moment.

"Hello?" said Ridley.

"You sound intelligent," Maddox said with a smile in his voice. "I'm waiting to see if you get it."

"Hold on..." said Ridley.

"Uh huh..." Another smile in the voice.

Ridley opened his eyes and leaned forward in his chair. "The timeline."

"Yup," said Maddox. "We found out Mehmet was killed. And we found out that his death preceded his brother's."

"So that couldn't have been him traveling to America," said Ridley.

"And so we have a third party on our hands," said Maddox. "And we're back to that Elia person."

"Any records in New York with that name?"

"Well," said Maddox, "if you were a guy traveling under nefarious circumstances under an assumed name, and that name has a trail of nefarious stuff associated with it, would you continue to use it?"

"I guess not."

"Right, because you're smart. This guy wasn't. He used the name again and again. We finally tracked him down. He recently rented a red SUV under his real name – Lorenzo Matteo. The car had a built-in GPS, so we were able to track where it was. Matteo obviously didn't think of that. Not only did his car trace the route of Jofar Aslan's murder, but it also led us to a restaurant where he paid for a meal with a credit card."

"Was the card under Matteo or the other name?"

"Neither," stated Maddox.

"Come again?"

"The card he used belonged to a certain *Beatricia Nespoli.*"

Something in Ridley's chest froze and tightened. He felt his jaw go slack.

"Hello?"

"Yeah," said Ridley, "still here."

"Name ring a bell?"

"Um, yeah, it does actually."

"I thought it might. It's the only name we've come across that connects all the dots."

"How so?" said Ridley, his mind still reeling.

"Oh," said Maddox, a small chuckle in his voice, "I almost forgot. The name *Beatricia Nespoli* is an anagram of *Elia Price-Bastino.*"

"And that other phrase," Ridley said as if in a daze.

"*Polite arabs in ice*, yes," replied Maddox. "Now, Beatricia Nespoli *is* a real name. Traceable. She's a real person. She's also clean as a whistle. Unlike her alias, who's left quite a trail of petty crime. So we talked to this guy Matteo. Boy, did he sing. We were able to trap him pretty quickly. He confessed to killing Jofar in a heartbeat. But he also gave up Nespoli. Said she paid him to do it. Gave him a card for expenses and credentials for getting around. Quite a large operation for a contract killing."

"Yeah," was all Ridley could say.

"Yeah," repeated the cop. "Now, here's the really disturbing part of the whole mess. Jofar is a foreigner, so is Matteo, so is Nespoli. When I took all this stuff to my chief, he told me I needed to check with the Italian and Turkish governments for extradition. A lot of red tape there. Fortunately — and here's the disturbing part — fortunately, Nespoli has credentials with the U.S. government."

"I know," Ridley said calmly.

"Some time ago she was assigned a position in U.S.–Vatican relations. Some sort of outreach thing. 'Bridging the ecumenical gap' was the phrase we kept hearing about. President Zimmer had reached out to Pope Leo XIV while he was campaigning for re-election. Something about a separation of Church and State initiative. They wanted to make peace with the Vatican in case they thought he was ostracizing them. Nespoli was something of an ambassador. She holds a doctorate in Comparative Religion. So far, that's the only qualification I can find. She minored in political studies. We think that's probably what brought her into contact with our government officials. So, as you might have guessed already, we called the White House. They put me on hold for what seemed like a day and a half, and when they finally got back on, they gave me your contact number."

Ridley took a deep breath, exhaling loudly into the phone. "Ok then."

"So I guess the ball is now in your court," said Maddox, echoing the breath. "I have to say, I'm relieved. Wait! My God, I can't believe I almost forgot! The church where Jofar was standing when Matteo ambushed him."

"What about it?"

"I think I found out what he was looking for. There was this phrase written inside, on the actual masonry of the place. Hard to explain. But I got a hunch that's what he was after. Got a pen?"

The detective dictated the Latin pangram.

"Got it," said Ridley, staring at the apparent gibberish.

"Mean anything to you?"

"No, not exactly."

"Not even without the Greek letters?"

"No."

Right after he said it, Ridley felt a surge inside himself. The cold, tight spot within him suddenly warmed, loosened. He started to laugh uncontrollably.

"Um," said Maddox, "sir?"

"I'm sorry," said Ridley, composing himself. But the fire inside him blazed. "Thank you, Detective Maddox. Can I call you at this number if I need you?"

"Sure thing, Mr. Shane."

"Ridley."

"Goodbye."

"Bye," said Ridley. His mouth felt permanently shaped into a smile. He looked at the Latin scrawl and laughed again.

"*Thank you, God*," he whispered, a tear welling in his eye.

He needed to get back to Pope Leo and the Brothers.

The Latin scrawl laid before him... and then there was that disc with the key to the Nicene Cipher...

# VATICAN CITY

"Beatricia Nespoli is a double agent," he said plainly.

The pope sat behind his desk, his fingers tented in front of his chin. Brothers Gabriel, Fernando, and Hendrik stood around in a semicircle.

"It makes sense," said Brother Gabriel, "considering that she was the one who got the cipher key."

"Only part of it," said Ridley. "Your Eminence, you have the rest of it."

The pope's face changed, suddenly incredulous.

"That disc," said Ridley, "contains a series of characters, all different. Each one stands for a letter of the alphabet. However, it's not a simple substitution cipher."

"You mean like a cryptogram puzzle?" said Brother Hendrik.

"I mean it's not like that at all. The Nicene Cipher is a good old-fashioned book code. Each letter in the phrase given to me by Detective Maddox corresponds, in sequence, to a character on the disc. It starts with the serpent's head and winds around clockwise. Once you substitute each one of those runes with a letter, you have the key phrase of a standard Vignière cipher, a book code. You can then use it to decipher the letter from Saint Paul.

You have to know the key phrase, otherwise the whole thing is gibberish."

At this, there came a horrible mewling sound, like that of a sick animal. The hairs on Ridley's neck pricked up as he swung around and saw the cause of the noise just outside the office. A security guard had just caught the thing that made the noise, and now held it by the arm. It was a man, but barely so.

Pope Leo called out, "Bring him here."

The others were stunned. They were all familiar with Pope Leo's unflinching courage, but it never ceased to amaze them how his courage worked hand in hand with his compassion for people.

The security brought the man in and said, "I caught him wandering the grounds outside. He was looking for a way in. Says his name is Giacomo."

The man was dressed in the tatters of a cotton suit, stained with many dark splotches. His skin was pocked and scored with lesions, which oozed and stank. His whole body was a perversion of humanity, a disgrace, and he panted like something that was hunted.

He was wild-eyed, with the look of a man staring into a nightmare. Another stink came off him, that of bodily odor mixed with truck exhaust – the smell of a man wandering outdoors, without sleep for many nights.

The pope gave a signal to the guard, who in turn let go of his charge. The man ambled into the middle of the room, then fell onto his knees.

"What are you doing here, Giacomo?" demanded Ridley.

"I denied my master, and I ran from him in shame."

"What do you mean? Who is your master?"

"I cannot speak his name. But you know him. And you will know him by his righteousness."

"Knox?" asked Ridley.

The man looked at him pitifully. "How dare you name him with your unclean lips."

"You ran from him?"

The man stared ahead, replaying his own past. He nodded. "There was a... a breech... and I ran."

"Where is your master?"

Giacomo smiled a mouthful of black and yellow and broken teeth. "It's too late. The serpent's head is dangling from its neck."

He began to quake with convulsive laughter, noiseless, his eyes wide and tearing.

"What is that supposed to mean?" asked Ridley. He had the urge to crack the guy across the cheek. There was something inhuman about him.

"Everything is in motion," the man declared. "Everything. The viper's brood will be trampled, the nest burned. And from the ashes will rise..." he began to shake ecstatically, crying fierce tears as he did.

"Will rise... what?" prompted Ridley.

"*The Messiah.*"

At this point, Pope Leo arose from his desk and moved around the front. He was an imposing figure, looming like a lion over the man.

"Who is this Messiah to you?" he asked softly.

The man looked up at him, derision in his red and watered eyes. "He is... as uncommon a man as ever you'll meet. When he was born, the birds fell to earth and did not die. Instead, they got up and sang his name in unison. Where he treads, trees grow and bear fruit. And when he says the word, they wither."

"And what did this man do for you?" asked the pope.

Giacomo's face tightened, and his mouth dropped. It was a moment before he was able to speak. "He... gave me... life!"

"What do you mean *he gave you life?*" There was a contempt in his voice that Ridley had never heard before.

"I was dead once. He killed me."

"Explain yourself."

A scummy little smile smeared across his face. "I was a whore, Father, just like you."

Brother Hendrik moved forward. Only a grab of his elbow by Brother Gabriel stopped him from laying his thick hand across the man's face.

The pope glanced disapprovingly at Brother Hendrik, then turned his gaze upon the man.

"So," said the pope, "you were a whore."

"I ate of the flesh and drank of the blood. And I bade others do the same. I praised the evil creator, and in the same breath I shunned him. You remember, Father: *Inasmuch as ye have done it unto one of the least of these my brethren, ye have done it unto me...*"

"You were a priest," guessed Ridley, feeling a touch of pity for the man. For a moment, he'd seen through a crack in the impossible façade.

The man looked at him and smiled. "The Master sent me to hell. He showed it to me. He gave me food that opened my eyes and my soul. I experienced hell like no man has... has ever... experienced..."

Again, he was staring into something so awful that it couldn't be articulated.

"He tortured you," said Ridley.

"Treated my wounds."

"He gave you drugs."

"Fed me."

"Put you in shackles."

"Clothed me."

"Took away your soul."

"Saved me," the man said in ecstasy. "*Inasmuch as ye have done it unto one of the least—*"

"We heard it already," said Ridley impatiently. "Where is your Messiah?"

Giacomo shook his head slowly. "No."

"You obviously hated him enough to escape. Where is he?"

"I won't betray him to whores, blasphemers all."

At this, Ridley grabbed the man by his tattered collars and pulled him up. The man yelped, and Ridley brought his stinking face close to his own.

"You little dung beetle," he growled as Brother Gabriel grabbed at his arms to free the man. "You think you know torture? What Knox did to you was nothing compared to what --."

"*Ridley!*"

Ridley looked over at the pope, whose voice still echoed in his brain.

"Let him go."

Ridley let go of the man, who fell to his knees again, quaking. A fetid smell hit him; the man had soiled himself.

"He will..." began the man, "not leave one stone upon another..."

"Another quote from Scripture," said Brother Gabriel.

"Referring to the end of times," said Ridley, staring at the man's pitiful form. "Where is your master?"

"Whited sepulchers," said the man, quoting once again.

"Get some new material," said Brother Gabriel.

"Wait a minute," said Ridley, reading insight into the words. "Let him speak."

Giacomo's lips trembled. "Beautiful outward, but are within full of dead men's bones, and of all uncleanness."

Ridley thought for a moment. "Ye build the tomb of the prophets," he said, continuing the quote.

"And garnish the sepulchers of the righteous," said the man, finishing it.

"You know a place like that?" pressed Ridley, his voice now calm and collected.

He broke down and covered his face.

Ridley leaned down slowly, until he was face to face. In a voice like spun silk, he uttered one name: "*Salerno.*"

The man recoiled as if struck with a cup of acid, and yelped so pitifully that several of the Brothers crossed themselves. When he was out of breath, he fell over, out cold.

"What in the name of God?" asked Brother Gabriel.

"Knox is hiding inside the Salerno Cathedral. His headquarters. The meat packaging plant was just a ruse."

"Are you sure?"

"You saw how he reacted. This poor guy was kept in a place with dead man's bones. Held prisoner there. Tortured, brainwashed. Who knows why. Part of some sick experiment that Knox cooked up, probably to see if he could convert someone to true loyalty or something."

"But why Salerno?" inquired Brother Gabriel. "I mean, how did you know?"

"You recognized the quote?" asked Ridley.

"From Saint Matthew, of course, but the...." The monk stopped himself.

Ridley rubbed the top of his smooth scalp. "The only answers he gave when questioned about his master's whereabouts were quotes from Saint Matthew. Salerno Cathedral," he said, "is home to Saint Matthew's relics."

## ROME, ITALY

Ridley went back to his hotel room to shower and change clothes. There was something awkward in the notion of preparing for a siege the way one prepares for a dinner date. He pushed the strange thought from his mind. There was one word to describe his state of mind: hell-bent.

His phone alerted him to a text.

From Beatricia Nespoli.

His heart quickened at the sight of the name. Even more so when he read the message: "Will you meet me? You know the place."

And then the next text, five seconds later: "I love you."

He sat down on the edge of the bed. Considered a prayer. The words wouldn't come. He looked to his nightstand. There was his holster, and the grip of his handgun sticking out of it.

Reluctantly, he slid the weapon into his waistband.

---

HIS FOOTSTEPS ECHOED down the cavernous Parrocchia di San Gregorio VII. His heart was pounding. Silly to feel this way. It was sheer lunacy. Falling for a girl like this. Sweaty pits like he was a teenager about to call her up and ask her out. And the whole time, feeling the bulge of the pistol on his back. He reached back, and with a shaky hand, retrieved the weapon.

No sight of Beatricia.

He walked slowly, each step producing an ominous answer.

*"The Church will crumble,"* he said, his words drawing out in a long, steady reverberation that had the life span of an ocean wave. "I didn't forget your words, Beatricia. The Church will crumble. *I must keep that from happening. I must rid the Church of its foes.* How does it feel to hear them read back to you? You're good with words, Beatricia. You can make them mean two separate things. You're used to that. Double meanings, double lives. Two of everything. Even gods, right?"

He heard the sharp *shuck-chock* of a shotgun racking a shell.

He turned to see her above him. She was on the second level, with the organ pipes behind her.

"I'll shoot you from here," she said. "Drop the gun."

He let the gun fall to the floor, then slowed his walk, but didn't stop. "Rid the Church of its foes, huh?"

"I said stop right there."

"You meant a purge, didn't you? You want the Catholic Church burned to the ground. You're on *his* side. A Gnostic revolution. Once Knox is in charge, you purge the ranks of all the enemies to the new order. You meant rid the *new* Church of its foes."

"That's enough," she said sternly, not a hitch in her voice.

"Am I right? Can you at least tell me that?"

"I love you, Ridley Shane. I mean that."

"You have a nifty way of showing it."

"Alright," she said. "I am a Gnostic. But I am not with *him*. Knox is a lunatic. A psychopath with heinous delusions. But I need him."

"Now what? Doesn't the unwritten Hollywood rule say you have to kill me now that I know your plan?"

"Not all of it."

"Tell me more, then," he said, taking another step forward.

"Stop moving!"

He stopped.

"Damn you, Ridley. You made it so difficult. When I found out you were on the case, I knew I had to insert myself between it and you. I put myself on Zimmer's radar. I sold my skills, Ridley. You should have heard my pitch to the president."

"If he had the slightest idea you were playing both sides, he would've thrown your ass in Gitmo. And he will when he finds out, believe me."

"Not with the new order. We have a concordat in the works with the Russian and Turkish governments. There will be a new alliance, a new order, a new dawn, Ridley. A new world. The Church is back."

"Why'd you give me the disc with the cipher key?"

She chuckled. "You don't know?"

"I'm asking."

"You really are lacking in self-assurance. I gave it to you because I thought you'd win. The enemy of my enemy. Any more questions?"

"One more: Why did you kill Jofar Aslan?"

"I didn't."

"Sorry. You *had him killed*. Is that better?"

"Specificity is key, Ridley. No more ambiguity. Yes, he sold out my Mehmet. And so I killed him."

"Revenge."

"I told you I would get my revenge for Mehmet. Everything was out in the open, Ridley. You're too smart for your own good. Looking for secrets everywhere. There are no secrets. There never were. Everything was right there in the light."

His eyes moved around the church, looking for any advantage he could grab.

"I'm not afraid to kill you here, Ridley," she said. "I don't want to, but I will for the glory of the Father."

He looked up at her. "The rosary," he said.

"What about it?"

"The last time we met here, you were saying it. You still cling to your Catholicism."

A slight smirk appeared on her face as she reached into her shirt and yanked at something.

A snake-like loop fell to the floor by his feet and shattered.

He looked at it. It was a Gnostic cross, similar in appearance to an Egyptian ankh. The beaded remains of the necklace were still scattering away from him.

"It's a Gnostic rosary," she said.

"You don't seem too attached to it."

"I won't be needing it."

Resigning herself to her own mortality had chilled her words. Their coldness hit him square in the jaw.

Beatricia Nespoli had two things to live for: revenge and the installation of a Gnostic pope. She herself had taken care of the first, and now Ridley Shane stood in front of the second.

She lived now for Ridley's death. He wouldn't give it to her.

It was a simple solution, as plain to him as anything: Live, and keep on living.

He began to laugh.

"What's so funny?"

"You're a smart girl, Beatricia. Real smart."

The laughter overtook him. It was a moment before he could compose himself.

"I hope you're enjoying yourself," she said.

"I am. Really. I mean, your sole mission in life now is to kill me, right? Which means that as long as I'm alive, you have something to live for? Which means that you can't kill me. You won't. You *need* your mission in life. You're caught in your own paradox, honey. I'll be seeing you."

With this, he jogged a few steps forward until he was directly under her, then he slowed his pace and began to whistle.

"Ridley!"

"See you around."

He listened carefully to her frantic steps above him as he exited through the side door.

Without another word, he left the church and ran down the block to his car. She wasn't stupid enough to fire at him out here. Still, he was quick about it.

He got into his car and a text lit up his phone. It was from Brother Gabriel.

"Old Man down need backup."

He put the vehicle in gear and tore back toward the Papal Palace.

## VATICAN CITY

He could see black smoke billowing out of one of the windows as he pulled up. Uniformed men – Vatican police – were running every which way. One over here, stopping mid-track, stooping to fire, resuming the charge; another one here, running toward the building, waving a couple of men behind him to follow. It looked as if the place was part of some messed-up snow globe tableau, and someone had given it a shake.

Getting to this point had not been easy. He had to fumble for his credentials – there being a novice guard left to man the gate during the chaos.

In the distance, he heard the sharp putter of a helicopter. Either the news or the military. A policeman came out of the building, spotted him, stooped, and fired. What the hell? Ridley had ducked at the right time. The bullet shattered his windshield. He cut the vehicle to the left and stepped on the gas pedal, running it up onto the sidewalk and part of the manicured lawn, clipping a birdbath along the way. He stopped the car and got out, the same cop had followed him. Ridley held up his hands, waving his CIA credentials.

"U.S. Government," he yelled. "Ridley Shane, CIA!"

The cop stopped about twenty yards away from him. Listened as he repeated his identification.

He took aim again.

Ridley dove behind the car. He heard the sound of bullets perforating the other side of the automobile. *What the hell?* Did the cop not hear him?

"*Shane!*" said a voice.

He looked up to see Brother Hendrik's head sticking out of a window on the second story. The monk was lowering a rope.

In an adjacent window was another figure. Brother Fernando. He pulled his head in, and a moment later there was the sound of gunfire coming from that very spot. Ridley turned to see the policeman who'd been shooting at him go down. Brother Fernando was an ace marksman.

"Get up here," yelled Brother Hendrik. "Fernando's got you."

With all the speed and agility he could muster, Ridley jumped onto the rope and scaled the wall of the palace like a lumbering monkey. Brother Hendrik grabbed hold and yanked him through the window. He landed with a thud, half on the monk, half on the tiled floor.

He looked around. They were in a mini-parlor. Ridley hadn't remembered ever setting foot in this part of the palace.

"OK," Ridley panted, "you have ten seconds to tell me what the hell's going on."

"A surge of police," said Brother Hendrik. "A stinking ambush."

"By the police?"

"I think only half of them are real cops. The other half are Knox's men, I'm guessing."

"I'll take your guess as gospel," said Ridley.

"Anyway, they stormed the place like the stinking Bastille. They took His Holiness away. God knows where."

Somewhere nearby, something exploded. Wood cracked and debris scattered.

"*Good God*," said Ridley.

"If you don't mind," said Hendrik, "we'll leave Him out of this one for now."

"Where are the others?"

"They're all up here on the second floor. We've been holding them off inside and out. It's stinking chaos. No one knows who's who. Police are shooting their own."

Another report, and another echoing wake of raining debris.

"They're tearing the place apart," said Hendrik.

"I thought I heard a helicopter before," said Ridley.

"No."

"No?"

"Listen, Ridley. We have no idea who Knox has paid off, who's out there working for him. If there's a helicopter on the way and it's his, our problems just got ten times worse."

"You're not talking surrender?"

Brother Hendrik looked sternly at him. "Not on your life. I'm talking fighting until the last breath. We ought to go out onto the floor at the top of the landing. It's a pretty good vantage point."

The idea put him in mind of Beatricia and her crow's nest position in the church only twenty minutes before.

They positioned themselves on either side of the balustrades and poked rifles through the slats.

"We can't communicate with anyone?" asked Ridley.

"There wasn't time to get a link up. It all happened so fast."

"I just had a date with Beatricia Nespoli," he said calmly. He felt Brother Hendrik's glare.

"Come again?"

"I'll tell you about it later, *when* we get out of this mess."

Three cops appeared at the bottom of the stairs, ostensibly having wandered in and lost their way.

"Hold it!" said Ridley. He wasn't keen on getting their attention, but rather keen on gauging their loyalty. Our side or theirs.

Upon spotting the two men, the three cops squatted and took aim.

Brother Hendrik fired, and Ridley followed suit. The three pseudo-cops dropped before getting off a single shot.

Another fake cop ambled into view. Upon seeing the bodies, he slowed even more, staring at them in horror. Taking advantage of the diversion, Ridley motioned for Hendrik to move so that each of them were at opposite ends of the balustrade which overlooked the receiving area below.

Ridley stood up, weapon aimed. "Don't move."

"Listen to him," said Hendrik, rising into view, weapon aimed at the man.

The man jerked his head to see Brother Hendrik, then back toward Ridley. He dropped his weapon. "Don't shoot," he said, his voice trembling.

"I want you to climb those stairs toward us. Slowly."

With this, Ridley moved to the top of the steps, weapon trained on the man the entire way.

As he neared the top, Hendrik also moved in. As he reached the final step, both men grabbed their prisoner and dragged him into the small parlor where Ridley had come in through the window.

They pulled the guy's arms behind him and secured his wrists with two zip ties. Then they took off his belt and used it to bind his ankles together. After making sure the man was securely trussed, Ridley grabbed the rope he'd used to scale the wall. The grappling hook was still firmly embedded below the sill. He tied it into a slip knot, put it over the man's head, and slid the knot tight against his throat. The man's eyes bulged in horror and he began to plead.

Ridley and Brother Hendrik picked him up despite his

screaming protests. His body flailed like an airborne salmon. They put him out the window, feet-first, facing inward, and lowered him carefully until they could just hold his body under the arms, his top half barely inside the window.

"Now shut up," Ridley grunted. The weight of the body was making his muscles tremble. "You've got a chance to save yourself from a pretty grisly death. Where did they take the pope?"

The man said nothing, merely grunted in return.

"I'm not sure how much longer I can hold you," he warned. "And I wouldn't put much faith in my friend here. He's not as strong as he looks." He felt Hendrik's glare at him.

The man began to pray.

"That's it," said Ridley. "We're dropping you on the count of three. One... two..."

The guy sang sweetly then. "They took the old man to Salerno."

Over the course of the next few minutes, they were able to use this little plan of Ridley's to great effect -- threatening to hang the guy, pulling him back, threatening to hang him again. By the end, they didn't need to exaggerate their inability to hold him.

After all was said and done, they were able to determine that the pope had been taken to Salerno, that Knox was there with him, that they had the cipher, and that the man who would replace the pope went by the name "Father Dietrich Severn".

They trussed the guy under the arms with the slack of rope that hung from his neck, and gently lowered him out the window until all the slack rope was taken up. The man dangled there – perfectly safe, just immobile – and in an incredibly inconvenient situation.

The men then left the room to join the others.

They soon got everyone accounted for and convened in the mini parlor.

"Is that..." began Brother Fernando, walking over to the

window. "Huh," he said matter-of-factly, "there's a guy hanging out there."

Brother Gabriel walked over. "Friend of yours?"

"Never mind him," said Ridley irritably. "Now, the way I see it, we have a palace full of men who may be cops or Knox's guys. Who knows? All I know is at this point, I'm done trying to figure it out. The pope's been taken to Salerno. As far as I'm concerned, that's our next stop. Who's with me?"

Not one of the Brothers objected.

"We have one problem," said Ridley.

"How to get out," said Brother Gabriel.

"Alright, two problems."

"What's the other?"

"I want to get the disc out of His Holiness's private safe. I don't suppose he has entrusted any of you with the combination or its whereabouts for that matter."

"I don't know the combination," said Brother Gabriel, "but I know where it is."

"That's a start," said Ridley.

"Yeah, a start. But it's on the other side of the palace. We have an army of cops fighting each other down there. And we're gonna make it all the way to the east wing without encountering a single one on either side of the fight?"

"Can you open the safe?"

Gabriel reached into his pocket and pulled out a small case the size of a ring box. "I think I can manage," he said, peeling open the box and revealing a tiny lump of what looked like orange Silly Putty.

"Semtex or C4?" said Ridley.

"Semtex," said Gabriel. "I've got wires in my kit."

"Then we're splitting up. Gabriel and I will head to the east wing and get the disc. Brothers Hendrik and Fernando will climb out this window and get a head start to Salerno. We'll keep in touch by cell phone until we can get radios for the rest of us."

Fernando gestured toward the window, then turned back to Ridley. "Three problems."

Hendrik stepped forward. "Gimme a hand." He and Fernando pulled the moaning soldier up into the room.

"Hey, pal," said Hendrik, "can we trust you to stay put up here?"

The man nodded weakly.

Hendrik looked at Ridley, then back. "Pal, I'm sorry about this. I really am." He then hauled off and laid a right cross at the man's jaw. The guy went out, colder than Christmas.

"See you in Salerno," said Hendrik. And the men split up.

---

THANK GOD, thought Ridley when he saw the safe. It was located in the pope's private room, positioned behind a portrait of the holy man's mother.

Thank God no one had looted here yet.

The men heard choppers in the distance. The military was definitely stepping in. Ridley had no intention of being here when they dropped down. Too many questions.

Brother Gabriel quickly molded a tiny lump of the Semtex no bigger than a canine tooth, stuck it to the safe lock, then deftly inserted two wires into it. He then ran the wires to a small battery pack, which he placed on the floor, and inserted the lead wires from a tiny remote-control device he held in his hand. The detonator was the size of a key fob.

Ridley turned his head as the blast sent bits of shrapnel showering around them. The safe lock had broken away like china.

Inside the safe was the disc with the key to the cipher and nothing else.

"Huh," muttered Ridley, "you suppose he had the foresight to know not to store this thing near other valuables?"

"The man is pretty sharp," said Brother Gabriel.

"Yeah, you think? Come on. Fernando's got some useful items in his room in the papal apartments. I got some stuff back at the hotel. If we hustle, we can make it outta here before the shit really comes down."

The route to the papal apartments was littered with bodies. More and more *polizia* were pouring in, and the more they did, the more confusion reigned. A helicopter landed, and then another touched down. Military personnel swarmed the place. The men barely made it to the apartments. Having loaded up with every bit of equipment they thought they might need, they procured a Hummer from a stunned soldier and took off.

The Vatican was now under martial law. The Hummer was stopped three times on the way out. Each checkpoint aroused more suspicion than the last, even though Ridley bore the most trusted credentials of anyone in this tiny little country.

When they finally made it outside of the Vatican wall, Ridley took a deep breath and let it go slowly. It was now 7:30 pm. Salerno was at least two and a half hours away. That gave Ridley barely enough time to formulate a plan of siege on the *Duomo*, as it was known.

It was a good thing Brother Gabriel was driving.

## SALERNO, ITALY

It was ten o'clock in the evening by the time they reached the Duomo di Salerno. Nestled within an assembly of tightly crammed apartment buildings and small businesses, the church could have easily been mistaken for a complex of state offices. Only the dead gray brick bell tower rising to twice the height of the tallest edifice in the area distinguished it among its fellows, situated as it was within the scattering of piazzas and winding, worming roads.

At this time of night, on a weekday, the silence hung wetly in the air. The hum of their vehicle was the only thing that signified to Ridley that this was not some mystical realm he was entering. He'd parked two blocks away behind a shop that sold lighting fixtures, in a narrow space that was cleaner than any alleyway he'd seen back home.

Loaded with equipment, Ridley and Gabriel moved stealthily along the twisting streets, keeping tabs on Hendrik's cell phone via GPS. Ridley touched the pocket on the sleeve of his flak jacket, and felt the disc resting snugly within.

Two forms loomed in the black street ahead of them. Ridley's cell phone lit up with a text.

*I see you, Kemo Sabe.*

Good ol' Hendrik.

They met up in the middle of the street, and Ridley equipped them without speaking a single word. Ridley motioned for them to follow him to the north side of the church, which faced the narrowest lane of all its sides. The walls that formed the inner atrium were at least sixty feet high.

Ridley stepped aside to allow Fernando access. Aiming a miniature cannon the size of his arm, the wiry Latino fired a pneumatic blast, launching a grappling hook that cleared the wall in one shot. The titanium metal claw hooked with a slight bit of retraction.

"Sure we're not gonna wake up the neighborhood?" whispered Hendrik.

"What's the big deal?" replied Fernando, whispering as well. "We're just a bunch of guys climbing the wall of an ancient church at night." He winked at his fellow monk, then hopped onto the line and began scaling the wall of the atrium.

Ridley's heart was in his throat watching the spider-like Fernando in action. As he receded from view, there was a painful few minutes of silence. Ridley's mind went wild with speculation; everything from Fernando's body hitting the ground at his feet to some loud alarm sounding.

In time, however, the line began to rise before them. Fernando was retrieving it from atop the wall. It would be another couple minutes before he appeared at the main entrance, looking as cocky as a frat boy.

He made a corny gesture like a fancy hotel doorman waving in a diplomat. Ridley patted him on the shoulder as he passed. He wanted to hug the guy.

The atrium was a fantastic bit of architecture, worthy of the description, "Romanesque". The magnificent courtyard was surrounded by portico archways supported by twenty or thirty massive columns. If he hadn't known any better, Ridley would have sworn he'd just walked straight through some rip in the space-time continuum, finding himself situated in medieval Italy. The church had been built in the eleventh century, and he had the eerie feeling that nothing had changed *at all* since then.

The men padded across the courtyard. Half through, Ridley stopped and turned to the rest.

"What is it?" asked Brother Gabriel.

"It's too quiet."

"I could have told you that."

But just as Ridley was about to respond, another idea had rolled over that one: this was a lot like the ambush back at La Chiesa San Pietro Damiani in Lazio. Right down to the sojourn into the crypts.

"I don't like this," he said. "We shouldn't be going straight up the middle. One or two of us should be coming around the rear. Three of us even."

"A little late for that now, isn't it?" joked Hendrik.

Ridley shot the burly monk a look.

"Just getting you back for that 'not as strong as he looks' comment back at the palace," Hendrik said with a wink.

Ridley suddenly became aware of the disc in his sleeve pocket. He touched it, then got an idea. With a new resolution, he bade the rest follow him into the church.

The interior of the church outdid the grandeur of its exterior.

White archways surrounding the nave rose to dizzying heights all around them. Within the apses on the opposite end were vivid, medieval mosaics, brightly-hued. On the north side, nearly camouflaged within the wall, was a door.

Glimpses of the ambush at Lazio flashed once more through Ridley's mind as he led the men through the door and down into the crypt.

Nothing prepared any of them for what they were about to lay their eyes on. The room sparkled with gilt-columns and walls, and Baroque designs on pillars. Everything was dazzling to the eyes in every direction and glowed with heavenly fire.

Here was where the relics of Saint Matthew lay. And here was where the poor soul Father Giacomo was tortured. But how could that be, when the place was a tourist attraction year-round?

Ridley looked carefully, trying desperately to notice minute details in the scant lighting provided by the emergency lamps.

Then he saw it, by the grace of God, he thought: a break in the diamond-shaped pattern on the floor. He tapped his foot on it, then scuffed it with the toe of his boot. It nudged ever so slightly.

Brother Fernando pulled out a multi-tool and flipped open a small, steel crowbar. This he jammed into the tiny crevice revealed by Ridley's scuffing of the tile. It gave, and the men crouched and pried a heavy three-by-three-foot panel up off the floor. A small series of wooden steps led down into the abyss.

Ridley tore open the pocket on his sleeve and pulled out the disc.

"Knox!" he yelled, his voice gruff and sharp. "I got it. The key to the cipher. And I know how to use it." He looked at the Brothers, all of them waiting for a response from the blackness.

"Knox!" he called again. "Come on up here and face us like a man. You have the Nicene Cipher, we have the key and the knowledge of how to use it. That's two against one, Knox."

A white face appeared out of the inky dark below. And a head trailed it, caught in the crook of an arm. The stoic face of Pope Leo was revealed there. Only the eyes had life, and they were weary and pleading.

"I have your nasty old pope," said Knox. "He smells like flowers. You know that? I never met a man who smelled like flowers before."

"Let him go, Knox," said Ridley.

"Oh, I'm afraid I can't do that, my friend. You see, I've won. Two against one? No. Two against, mmm, three."

Another figure appeared and ascended the steps, and Ridley found himself once again face to face with Beatricia Nespoli.

"Hello, Ridley," she said coldly.

Ridley shook his head. "I didn't think you could sink any lower. What kind of woman are you?"

"Not your type, I guess."

He looked into her eyes. They stared dead ahead, dilated. She was gaunt, and looked as though she wanted to cry but had forgotten how to do it.

"I'm ruined, Ridley," she said flatly. "I couldn't be your type if I tried."

Ridley caught a lump in his throat as the truth of the situation hit him. "Knox, you piece of dirt. You drugged her."

"She's mine, friend," said the demented Messiah.

"No. You're done, Knox."

Knox chuckled. "Done? I was put on this earth to help humanity find its way home, heathen. This twisted liar knows it in his heart, don't you?" He gave Pope Leo's neck a slight squeeze, causing the man to wince. "I'm here to turn you away from the evil god and bring you to the Father of the Redeemer. I've got a pope of my own, you know, all ready to take his place. And I got a clutch of cardinals ready to vote him in. It's the new order, son, and I'm its Messiah."

With this, he yanked Pope Leo's body so that the Holy Man served as Knox's human shield.

"*I believe*..." said Pope Leo.

Knox loosened his arm lock on the old man's neck. "What's that, you ol' bugger?"

"I believe..." Pope Leo gasped, "in one God, the Father Almighty, maker of Heaven and Earth..."

"Hey," said Knox, "shut the hell up, please? I'm trying to talk here."

Pope Leo's voice broke and trembled with tears. "And in one Lord Jesus Christ, the only-begotten Son of God, begotten of the Father. God of God, Light of Light, true God of true God, *begotten and not made...*"

At this, Knox burst into a fit of raucous laughter. "Now wouldya listen to that? Sing it for me, son!"

"Ridley," pleaded His Holiness, tears streaming down his cheek. "Do what you have to do."

"Now look," said Knox, suddenly regaining his composure. "My mama may have been a no-good piece of crusted crap hanging off the back end of an armadillo in August, but she certainly didn't raise—"

Knox's face had no time to register what his eyes saw at that moment. And what they saw was Ridley Shane crouch, aim his pistol...

The bullet tore through the pope's shoulder and exploded through Knox's head. The pope fell away with an agonized scream. Knox's lifeless body fell beside him.

Brother Fernando grabbed Beatricia while Ridley and the other Brothers jumped down the steps into the darkness. A single candle illuminated the ten-by-ten-foot pit, and caught the glimmer of chains hanging from the ceiling, a tray with hooks and knives, and bloodied instruments that looked like they belonged in a medieval barber shop. The place smelled like rotting earth, and was tinged with something... unholy.

And there was no one else down here.

Evil had stamped its foul mark on this place forever.

## VATICAN CITY, FOUR WEEKS LATER

Brothers Aaron and Zigfried were released and convalescing in the papal apartments. It wasn't long before the roommates were debating the meaning of religious texts with all the zeal and lighthearted ribbing that they couldn't live without.

His Holiness was coming along with the strength of a bull. Press releases stated that he was admitted to the hospital with an undisclosed illness; then updated today to say that the condition was not life-threatening and that he'd been released. The office had to employ extra help handling all the extra get well wishes and cards pouring in from all over the globe.

Ridley, who'd stayed on for an extra month to oversee the cleanup and monitor the PR, now paced the foyer, speaking in hushed tones on his cell phone.

"I'm fine, really."

"Why don't I believe you?" said President Brandon Zimmer.

"Because you're a politician and you don't have faith in anything."

"Geez, fair enough."

Ridley was silent for a moment, unsure of how to ask the president what he needed to ask him.

"She'll be OK," said the president.

"What's that?"

"Beatricia. That's who you were going to ask me about, right?"

Ridley drew a strong breath. "Maybe."

"Well, I'm not gonna lie. Knox really did a number on her. Kept her plied with drugs. Brainwashed her. She started off this whole thing hell-bent on finding her boyfriend's killer. But somewhere along the line, I don't know, I guess she snapped. We're trying to get to the bottom of it. But she'll pull through alright. That's what the doctors said."

"What about the other guy?"

"Other guy?"

"Dietrich Severn. The ringer pope."

"Still at large, I'm afraid. The Hand of Marcion splintered. But these things have a way of gluing themselves back together right under your nose. We're keeping an eye out."

"Severn's out in the cold then. That sucks."

"We'll get him," said the president. "But I've got a feeling, based on the intel report you sent, that he's kept his hands pretty clean. We might be able to get him on being an accessory before the fact. While we're on that subject, no clue on the whereabouts of the Nicene Cipher, huh?"

"No," said Ridley. "I mean, if I had to guess, I would say Severn made off with it. That's just a hunch."

"Well, we'll certainly make it a point to ask him about it when we get him, don't you worry. Ridley, how are *you*?"

"You asked me that already."

"Before I meant physically."

"Well, sir, to be honest," said Ridley, "I don't know. I came here expecting a bunch of routine intelligence work. I wound up a wannabe action hero."

"Well," said the president, "you've done an outstanding job. I want you to take a nice long vacation. On my dime. And then I'd like you to consider relocating."

"Relocating?"

"That detective, the one who investigated the Aslan murder here, name's Maddox? He lives in a town on the north shore of Long Island. A little place called Tillings Neck. Word on the street is that they could use a little help."

"You're reassigning me to Mayberry?"

"Not exactly. We've heard some chatter. Jofar Aslan had a lot of little side projects going on. Some of those are taking root. We think Tillings Neck might be the home base for a domestic terrorist cell. I think the change would be good for you. And I think you're capable of handling it."

"Why me?"

The president chuckled. "You, my friend, are one of the only people who can get away with asking a question like that of your Commander in Chief. Well, I'll tell you. I need a guy with a strong compass. A guy who understands right and wrong, and knows that the law doesn't always accommodate the moral gauge of nature."

"I think I know what you mean."

"How does that sound?"

"I guess I don't have a choice. I go where my president needs me."

"That's what I like to hear. Hang in there, Ridley."

"Goodbye, Mr. President."

He walked slowly to the pope's private room on the second floor of the palace. The workmen had made significant progress. A great deal of the floor needed to be replaced. Walls repaired. Lighting fixtures replaced. Everywhere one turned, there was the ugly stamp of human beings at their worst.

The pope's private secretary, a young man by the name of Johann, smiled at Ridley as he approached. Without a word, he knocked twice on the door of the pope's room and then entered. A moment later, he emerged and gave Ridley entrance.

The pope lay propped up in his bed, his bandaged shoulder fully visible. He, like the palace itself, was coming along just fine.

"Please," he said, gesturing to a chair by the bed. "I've got a gift for you." He reached toward the nightstand on his right. From its drawer, he produced a small box and offered it to Ridley. "Open it."

Ridley did as he was told. It was a beautiful gold necklace with a pendant attached.

"It's beautiful," said Ridley. "Thank you."

"You've held it before. It's the piece that held the runes, the key to the Nicene Cipher."

Ridley felt his own eyes widen. "But..."

"I had it melted down and reformed into that."

"Yes, but... I don't know what—"

"Ask."

Ridley thought for a moment. "What is the truth?"

The pope smiled. "That was the right question, as it should always be. The truth is what is."

Ridley nodded. "What is it?"

The pope's smile grew larger. "*The truth is what is*. It's a quote from Lenny Bruce," said the pope.

"The old comedian?"

The pope nodded. "Someone told it to me long ago. I remembered it recently. God has written the truth on your heart, Ridley. Defend that, and you defend Him."

"So, you're saying it doesn't matter that we may have destroyed a part of something that could have been true."

"What do you mean?"

"This." He held up the pendant that was once the runic disc. "This could have decoded a document that was the word of the Lord, am I wrong? Can we live with that?"

"Was it written on your heart?"

"No, but..."

"Therefore, you had no reason to defend it."

"But Knox... and the Gnostic militants... and what about every religion that—"

He stopped himself when he realized what he was actually saying.

The pope explained. "Men and women kill each other over the meaning of words. We cannot question why that is. But we can say that every man and woman is endowed by God with the right to defend the truth He has written on their hearts. That is the only thing that matters. We will be judged for how we do it, not why we do it."

Ridley bowed his head and took a deep breath.

"You didn't read the inscription on the pendant," said the pope.

"Sorry?"

His Holiness pointed to the necklace.

Ridley picked it up and turned it over. It was a Latin phrase: *Vocatus atque non vocatus, Deus aderit.*

"It's a quote from Erasmus," said the pope. "Say the words in English. I want to hear them on your tongue."

Something caught in Ridley's throat, and it was a moment before he could speak without his voice breaking. "Called or not called, God will be there."

"Yes. More loosely translated it means: *whether or not you ask for Him, God is present.* And there is something else you came to see me for."

"I came to say goodbye."

The pope smiled. "You mean, 'so long'."

Ridley nodded. "So long."

The pope's face grew serious. "But that isn't what I was referring to."

Ridley's mouth went dry, and he fought his tears.

"It's OK, my child," said Pope Leo.

Ridley Shane cleared his throat. Then he bowed his head and crossed himself. "Bless me Father, for I have sinned..."

I hope you enjoyed this story.

**If you did, please take a moment to write a review on Amazon.** Even the short ones help!

**>> GET A FREE COPY OF THE CORPS JUSTICE PREQUEL SHORT STORY, *GOD-SPEED*, JUST FOR SUBSCRIBING AT HTTP://CG-COOPER.COM <<**

# ALSO BY C. G. COOPER

**The Corps Justice Series In Order:**

*Back To War*

*Council Of Patriots*

*Prime Asset*

*Presidential Shift*

*National Burden*

*Lethal Misconduct*

*Moral Imperative*

*Disavowed*

*Chain Of Command*

*Papal Justice*

*The Zimmer Doctrine*

*Sabotage*

*Liberty Down*

*Sins Of The Father*

**Corps Justice Short Stories:**

*Chosen*

*God-Speed*

*Running*

**The Daniel Briggs Novels:**

*Adrift*

## ABOUT THE AUTHOR

C. G. Cooper is the *USA TODAY* and AMAZON
BESTSELLING author of the CORPS JUSTICE novels
(including spinoffs), The Chronicles of Benjamin Dragon and the
Patriot Protocol series.

Cooper grew up in a Navy family and traveled from one Naval
base to another as he fed his love of books and a fledgling desire
to write.

Upon graduating from the University of Virginia with a degree in

Foreign Affairs, Cooper was commissioned in the United States Marine Corps and went on to serve six years as an infantry officer. C. G. Cooper's final Marine duty station was in Nashville, Tennessee, where he fell in love with the laid-back lifestyle of Music City.

His first published novel, BACK TO WAR, came out of a need to link back to his time in the Marine Corps. That novel, written as a side project, spawned many follow-on novels, several exciting spinoffs, and catapulted Cooper's career.

Cooper lives just south of Nashville with his wife, three children, and their German shorthaired pointer, Liberty, who's become a popular character in the Corps Justice novels.

When he's not writing or hosting his podcast, Books In 30, Cooper spends time with his family, does his best to improve his golf handicap, and loves to shed light on the ongoing fight of everyday heroes.

Cooper loves hearing from readers and responds to every email personally.
*To connect with C. G. Cooper visit*
www.cg-cooper.com

Made in the USA
San Bernardino, CA
22 May 2020